DAILY LOG

Re: Alliance Trust case

Picked up witness today and brought her to a safe house. For her own protection, she is in disguise. No one will ever know who she is. I hardly recognize the woman myself.

With her here, it's harder to keep my identity secret from my family, but I have no choice. It's the only way I can operate for the agency.

Hot on the heels of the embezzler, thanks to the data our mole downloaded. Expect to close the case by month's end. My inquiries have uncovered some disturbing evidence, however. If I'm right, we can trust no one.

Just in case, I'm keeping my witness next to me at all times. Must admit, with this beauty, it's no hardship. Have to keep reminding myself she's just an assignment.

No matter what, I'll use whatever resources my money can buy to keep her safe.

—Casanova

Dear Reader,

I was so thrilled to return to the Silhouette Desire line after a ten-year hiatus, and I feel so lucky to participate in THE ELLIOTTS continuity with so many of Desire's star authors. But once I was assigned my characters, I was over the moon, because the story included so many of my favorite elements—a little bit of *My Fair Lady,* mixed in with a touch of suspense and food. Talk about heaven! I also got to dabble a bit in fashion (not my forte in real life, so I enjoyed Lucy's delicious clothes vicariously).

As a result of my research into restaurants and food preparation, I became very interested in gourmet cooking. And so, at the ripe old age of *mumble mumble* I am learning to cook! I've even taken a couple of classes.

Incidentally, the infamous orange-chocolate-mint cake that leads to some lascivious lovemaking is a completely fictitious concoction. But my goal is to eventually devise a working recipe! When I do, I'll publish it on my Web site, www.karalennox.com.

All best,

Kara Lennox

KARA LENNOX

Under Deepest Cover

Silhouette®

Desire

Published by Silhouette Books

America's Publisher of Contemporary Romance

For Melissa Jeglinski
Thanks so much for inviting me into the Elliott world.
The story was perfect for me—you know me well.

Acknowledgments
Special thanks and acknowledgment are given to
Kara Lennox for her contribution to
THE ELLIOTTS miniseries.

SILHOUETTE BOOKS

ISBN-13: 978-0-373-76735-9
ISBN-10:   0-373-76735-8

UNDER DEEPEST COVER

Visit Silhouette Books at www.eHarlequin.com

Printed in U.S.A.

Books by Kara Lennox

Silhouette Desire

Under Deepest Cover #1735

Harlequin American Romance

Vixen in Disguise #934*
Plain Jane's Plan #942*
Sassy Cindedrella #951*
Fortune's Twins #974
The Millionaire Next Door #990
The Forgotten Cowboy #1052
Hometown Honey #1068††

Harlequin Intrigue

Bounty Hunter Ransom #756†
Bounty Hunter Redemption #805†
Bounty Hunter Honor #853†

*How To Marry a Hardison
†Code of the Cobra
†† Blond Justice

KARA LENNOX

The Texas native has been an art director, typesetter, textbook editor and reporter. She's worked in a boutique, a health club and an ad agency. She's been an antiques dealer and even a blackjack dealer. But no work has made her happier than writing romance novels.

When not writing, Kara indulges in an ever-changing array of weird hobbies. (Her latest passions are treasure hunting and creating mosaics.) She loves to hear from readers. You can visit her Web page and drop her a note at www.karalennox.com.

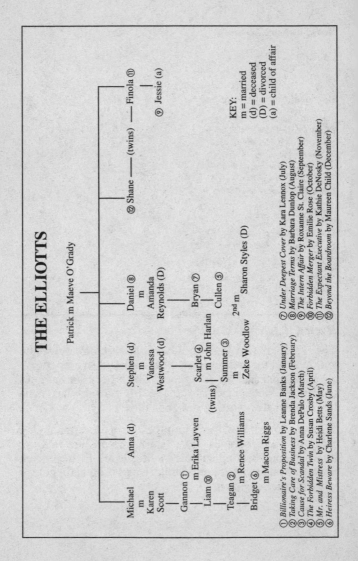

THE ELLIOTTS

Patrick m Maeve O'Grady

Michael
m
Karen
Scott

Anna (d)

Stephen (d)
m
Vanessa
Westwood (d)

Daniel ⑧
m
Amanda
Reynolds (D)

Shane ⑫ — (twins) — **Finola ⑪**

Gannon ①
m Erika Layven

Liam ⑩ ⎱ (twins)

Teagan ② ⎰
m Renee Williams

Bridget ⑥
m Macon Riggs

Scarlet ④ ⎱
| m John Harlan
Summer ③ ⎰
m
Zeke Woodlow

Bryan ⑦

Cullen ⑤
2nd m
Sharon Styles (D)

⑨ Jessie (a)

KEY:
m = married
(d) = deceased
(D) = divorced
(a) = child of affair

① *Billionaire's Proposition* by Leanne Banks (January)
② *Taking Care of Business* by Brenda Jackson (February)
③ *Cause for Scandal* by Anna DePalo (March)
④ *The Forbidden Twin* by Susan Crosby (April)
⑤ *Mr. and Mistress* by Heidi Betts (May)
⑥ *Heiress Beware* by Charlene Sands (June)
⑦ *Under Deepest Cover* by Kara Lennox (July)
⑧ *Marriage Terms* by Barbara Dunlop (August)
⑨ *The Intern Affair* by Roxanne St. Claire (September)
⑩ *Forbidden Merger* by Emilie Rose (October)
⑪ *The Expectant Executive* by Kathie DeNosky (November)
⑫ *Beyond the Boardroom* by Maureen Child (December)

One

"**Y**ou have to get me *out* of this!" Lucy Miller hissed into her encrypted cell phone, the one that had been delivered to her home a few weeks ago. The phone had rung just as she'd left a staff meeting. She'd ducked into the ladies' rest room, where she'd checked every stall to make sure she was alone.

"Relax, Lucy," said the soothing voice Lucy had come to know so well. She had often fantasized about what the man who owned that deep, sexy voice might look like, but not today. Today she was too terrified to fantasize about anything but getting out of this situation with her skin intact.

"Don't you tell me to relax," she whispered back. "You aren't the one stuck in this bank trying to act normal when she knows she's about to get liquidated."

"Liquidated? You must be watching too much *Get Smart.* No one is trying to kill you."

"You didn't see the man who was following me. I know a hit man when I see one. He was wearing a coat, and it's like ninety degrees outside."

"It's also raining in D.C. today. He probably had on a raincoat."

"Casanova, you're not listening! My cover has been blown. Someone has been in my apartment. Either you get me out of here, or I'll hop the first plane I can find to South America and I'll take all my data with me!"

"No! Lucy, be reasonable—"

"I'm done being reasonable. I've done everything you asked without question. I've trusted you implicitly, though I've never met you and don't even know your name. Now it's your turn to trust me. I'm not stupid. If you don't get me out, this very expensive little cell phone is going into the nearest sewer, and you'll never hear from me again."

"All right! I'll be there by five-thirty, six at the latest. Can you hang tight till then? Can you make it home?"

Lucy took a deep breath, trying to calm herself. She'd spotted her tail three days ago, and she'd realized yesterday that someone had searched her apartment. But so far her observer was keeping his distance. Maybe she could make it a few more hours. She struggled for a reasonable tone of voice. "I'll do my best. But if anything happens, tell my parents I love them, okay?"

"You'll be fine, drama queen."

Lucy disconnected before she said something she'd regret. Drama queen? Did Casanova think she was some flaky paranoid? Hadn't she proved her worth over the past weeks? Casanova. Who'd come up with that handle, anyway, and why?

She put the cell phone back in her purse and started to exit the rest room, but then she caught a look at herself in the mirror. She looked like a mad woman, her wavy brown hair escaping from its customary bun and frizzing around her face, her cheeks flush with panic, eyes wild with fear behind her glasses. She took five minutes to neaten her hair, powder her nose and apply her pink lipstick. The shade did nothing for her, but that didn't matter. She wasn't exactly supermodel material these days. She only wore a little makeup because she was in an executive position and the other female executives did.

She'd been trying to fit in, not call attention to herself.

When she looked and felt more composed, she left the sanctuary of the rest room and headed for her office, hoping she could close the door and hole up in there for the rest of the afternoon. She was afraid that if she had to deal with anyone, she would fall apart.

Some spy you turned out to be, Lucy Miller. Disintegrating at the first sign of danger.

As luck would have it, she rounded a corner and ran right into the bank's portly CEO, the man who'd hired her.

"Oh, hello, Lucy," he said politely. "I was just looking for you."

"Sorry, I was in the ladies' room. My lunch isn't sitting well, I'm afraid." She figured he wouldn't ask too many questions about that. He was easily embarrassed, she'd discovered.

He scrutinized her face with his one good eye. The other had been destroyed in some kind of accident, though she didn't know the details. Her skin prickled with nerves. Could he see her fear?

"You don't look well," he said. "You're very pale. Are you sure you're okay?"

"I'm fine, really." Just like Mr. Vargov to be concerned. He was a kind, fatherly man, a friend of her uncle Dennis who'd given her this job when she sorely needed a safe, stable employment. She'd been under-qualified for the fund auditor's job, with her piddling bachelor's degree in finance and no experience to speak of, but she felt she'd performed the job well.

Too well, in Mr. Vargov's opinion. He thought she was *too* conscientious. He hadn't taken her suspicions about embezzlement very seriously. That was why she'd gone to Homeland Security. That was how she'd gotten involved with Casanova.

"Why don't you take the rest of the afternoon off?" Mr. Vargov suggested.

"Oh, I couldn't. You said you wanted those reports—"

"The reports can wait. Your uncle would have my hide if he found out I was cracking the whip over you when you're sick."

"Thanks, Mr. Vargov. Maybe I will leave just a little early if I don't feel better."

"I think you should."

And maybe, she thought, if she left early, she could fool the man or men who'd been following her. She wouldn't mind saying goodbye to this place. She'd needed a place to recover, to heal, to get her bearings, and Alliance Trust had provided that. Her co-workers had been kind, the working conditions pleasant. Her boss hadn't required too much of her, and the salary had been much higher than someone her age and experience normally earned.

But it was time to move on. She would spend another

hour downloading as much information as she could onto her supercapacity memory stick, then leave here and never come back.

Casanova would take her to a safe house. He'd promised. And then, when all the arrests were made and the perpetrators were in jail, she could start over somewhere else. A new job, a new life.

It sounded like heaven.

At ten after three, she was ready. She stashed the memory stick in her bra. Taking only her purse and umbrella, she told Peggy Holmes, Mr. Vargov's executive secretary and the woman who knew everything, that she was going home early due to an upset stomach.

"Oh, my dear, I hope it's nothing serious. You've missed only one day of work since you started here, and that was for a root canal. On a lower-left molar, I believe." Peggy was in her sixties and had worked for Mr. Vargov for twenty-something years. With her tightly permed hair and dumpy, big-bosomed figure, she was everyone's grandmother. But Lucy knew she was highly intelligent with an astounding memory for detail and an efficiency that bordered on pathological.

"I'll be fine," Lucy said, hoping it was true.

The idea of walking into the parking garage alone held little appeal. One of the security guards would have been happy to escort her, but if a hit man was waiting for her there, she might just be dragging the guard into danger.

She shouldn't behave as expected, she decided. She would take the bus. There was a bus stop just a block from her office.

The weather was warm and humid with an insistent, light rain falling, but Lucy felt cold inside as she exited her building. She put up her umbrella, taking the opportunity to glance surreptitiously around to see if she spotted the man in the raincoat. But she saw no one suspicious.

She walked up the block, her sensible low heels tapping against the wet sidewalk. She pretended to window-shop, not wanting to stand at the bus stop too long. When she saw the bus approaching, she hurried to the stop and dashed onboard just in time. The only other people to board with her were a mom with two small children. Thank God.

When she got off at the stop near her Arlington, Virginia, town house, she still saw no one. Maybe she'd outmaneuvered him. Or maybe he'd given up on her, decided she was no one to worry about. He wouldn't have found anything incriminating in her home. She kept the memory stick with her at all times.

Her tiny town house had only one door, and this morning she'd rigged it so she would know if anyone had been inside. She checked; the tiny hair she'd caught between door and frame was still in place. She inserted her key and entered, pausing to close her wet umbrella and shake it off on the porch.

She'd lived here for two years. Her uncle had found it for her, and she'd committed to renting it without ever seeing it. It was nice but boring—like her life had been until a few weeks ago—and she'd made no effort to turn it into a real home. She wouldn't mind walking away from it.

As she closed and bolted the door, a hand clamped over her mouth and a strong arm hauled her against a rock-hard body.

Panic rising in her throat, Lucy didn't think, she just acted. The umbrella was still in her hand. She aimed it behind her and jabbed her attacker in the thigh as hard as she could.

Her attacker issued a strangled gasp and loosened his grip on her just enough that she could bend her knees and drop. As she did, she grabbed one of the man's denim-clad legs and yanked, throwing him off balance. He fell onto the marble floor with a painful-sounding thunk. Still gripping the umbrella, Lucy straightened, swiveled toward her attacker and went for his throat with the sharp tip of her impromptu weapon.

He grabbed the umbrella and deflected it. "Lucy, stop! It's me, Casanova!" He jerked the umbrella out of her hands and tossed it aside. Unfortunately, he also knocked her off balance. She fell on top of him and found herself staring into a pair of the most remarkable blue eyes she'd ever seen.

"Casanova?" But she knew it was him. She'd recognized his voice instantly.

"Jeez, woman, are you insane? You almost killed me."

"You broke into my home and attacked me, I fought back, but I'm insane?"

"You're not supposed to be home until later. I had no idea who you were. And where did you learn to fight like that?"

"I took a self-defense class. What are you doing in my house?"

"If you're under surveillance, I couldn't just come to the front door. I broke in."

"How? I have an alarm."

"Your neighbor doesn't." He grinned, and Lucy looked up and into the living room, where she saw a huge hole in her wall. "You came through the wall? You didn't frighten Mrs. Pfluger, did you? And what's my landlord going to say?"

"You won't be here to find out. We're leaving."

That was the first comforting thing he'd said. "Then you believe me?"

"Your house is riddled with more listening devices than the American Embassy in Russia. Someone's been here, all right." His expression turned grim.

Lucy dropped her voice to a whisper. "Are they listening? Right now?"

"My guess is the bugs are connected to a voice-activated recording device. They—whoever they are—probably aren't monitoring live when you're not supposed to be home. But we don't have much time. They'll catch up with you soon. I want to be long gone by the time they get here. So if you could, uh…"

Lucy was humiliated to realize she was still lying on top of him, and she hadn't made even a token effort to move. She could feel every hard-muscled inch of him pressed against her body, and she had to say the effect wasn't unpleasant. It had been a very long time since any man had touched her more intimately than with a handshake.

She scrambled off of Casanova, managing to knee him in the groin in the process, though not intentionally.

"Damn, woman, you're dangerous." He sat up and shook his head as if to clear it, and she got her first really good look at him. In all her fantasies he'd been handsome, but nothing had prepared her for the reality. He was *gorgeous*—six feet of highly toned body, thick, jet-black hair and those incredible eyes. His hair was all mussed from their impromptu romp, the way it might look if he'd just gotten out of bed.

Oh, Lucy. Knock it off.

"You've got exactly three minutes to pack anything you absolutely need. Medications, a toothbrush, change of underwear. Don't worry about clothes."

Lucy believed him. She ran into the bedroom, grabbed a couple of pairs of underwear and socks, her toothbrush and her allergy medicine. All of it could be tossed into a tiny backpack. Since she had a couple of minutes, she peeled off her skirt and sticky pantyhose and put on a pair of jeans and her running shoes. She didn't know where they would go, how they would travel or how long before they stopped, and she wanted to be comfortable.

She emerged from the bedroom with seconds to spare. Casanova was waiting for her, looking antsy, rolling up on the balls of his feet. "About time."

"You said three minutes, I took three minutes." Then she couldn't help it. She grinned.

"You're enjoying this."

"In a way," she admitted. It had been a very long time since she'd had adrenaline pumping through her veins and color in her cheeks. Years. She'd forgotten how good it felt. "And you enjoy it, too, or you wouldn't be a spy to begin with."

He nodded, conceding the point. "Let's go."

Casanova led Lucy through the hole he'd made in her sheetrock. "I'm glad Mrs. Pfluger wasn't home," she said. "You'd have probably scared her to death."

"What makes you so sure she isn't home?" And sure enough, sitting in the living room watching her TV was Lucy's neighbor, Mrs. Pfluger, who was eighty-two years old. She smiled at Casanova. "So, you're back," she said with a bright smile. Although she was nearly incapacitated with arthritis, her mind was as sharp as any twenty-year-old's. "Hello, Lucy, dear."

Lucy stared, dumbfounded. "Do you two know each other?"

"We do now," Mrs. Pfluger said. "He came to my door, and when he explained you were in danger from some terrorists, and that he needed my help so you could escape…" She shrugged helplessly, as if to say, Well, you know how these things are. Like they happened every day.

"But the wall. He ruined your wall," Lucy said.

"He handed me a wad of cash to pay for it." She turned back to Casanova. "Now, while you were busy searching Lucy's apartment, I gathered the things you would need." She gestured toward an old shopping bag. "They're clothes and other things from my fat days. I won't need them back."

Casanova inspected the contents of the shopping bag, then grinned and looked at Lucy. "Excellent. Lucy, put these things on. You're about to become Bessie Pfluger."

Bryan Elliott, aka Casanova, tried not to grin as he watched Lucy Miller wiggle into a pair of huge orange polyester stretch pants and pin them at the waist. She'd turned out to be a surprise.

He already knew a lot about her from the background information he'd obtained—where she grew up, where she'd gone to school, her employment history. He'd pegged her as the perfect mole to work inside Alliance where the embezzling was taking place—dutiful, conscientious, intelligent. And she was all those things. Over the past few weeks she had proved amazingly helpful, downloading tons of information onto the supercapacity memory stick, following his instructions without question.

In person, though, she was surprisingly feisty—and damned efficient at defending herself. With the proper training— No, he shouldn't even think about that. He'd let himself get sucked into a life of lies and shadows, and he was in so deep now he could never lead a normal life. He didn't wish that on sweet Lucy Miller, who, by all accounts, was ignorant of the uglier side of life.

But she was no longer ignorant about the ugliest clothes in the universe. She'd topped the orange pants with a tentlike housecoat with rainbows all over it. She'd tucked her hair up into a silver, curly-haired wig and donned an old pair of Mrs. Pfluger's glasses, which had red frames and were only slightly uglier than Lucy's own.

"My old walker is over there." Mrs. Pfluger gestured toward a corner of her living room.

"This will never work," Lucy said on a moan. "No one will believe I'm eighty years old."

"Eighty-two," Mrs. Pfluger said.

"Trust me, if anyone is watching the place, they won't look past the obvious at the place next door." He unfolded the portable walker and set it in front of Lucy. "Let's see you do an old-lady walk."

Lucy hunched over the walker and did a creditable imitation of an arthritic senior citizen inching along.

"Oh, heavens," Mrs. Pfluger said. "Please don't tell me I look like that when I walk."

"I'm exaggerating," Lucy said. Then she turned to her neighbor and gave her a spontaneous hug. "Oh, Mrs. Pfluger, I can't thank you enough for helping us out like this. I mean, you don't even know this guy."

"He showed me a badge," Mrs. Pfluger said innocently, having no clue the badge he'd shown her was fake and could be bought on any street corner in D.C. "Anyway, he has trustworthy eyes. He'll take care of you."

"I'm counting on it," Lucy said, giving Bryan a meaningful look. "Can we go now?"

Bryan thanked Lucy's elderly neighbor, too, then "helped" Lucy out the door and down the wheelchair ramp.

"Keep your head down. That's it," he whispered. "You're doing great. If I didn't know better, *I'd* swear you were someone's grandmother." But he did know better. The body that had been pressed against his when she'd fallen on him was not the slightest bit grandmotherly. In fact, he'd been surprised at how slim and firm she was beneath the frumpy suit she'd worn.

His Mercedes was parked at the curb. Knowing the town house might be under surveillance, he'd made no attempt to be stealthy, walking right up to the neighbor's door and ringing the bell. He'd known she would be home. He'd also known she'd been an army nurse in Korea and her husband had been a World War II veteran. He'd been counting on her patriotism to make her willing to help him out, and he'd been right.

As he usually was. He liked to cover all the bases.

As soon as the motor started and the car was underway, he relaxed slightly. If anyone had been watching, Lucy's old-lady act had fooled them. No one was following.

Bryan drove to a mall parking lot and pulled the Mercedes into a spot fairly close to where he'd found it.

"Why are we stopping here?" Lucy asked.

"Switching cars." He turned off the engine and pulled his Multi-Key from the ignition.

"What is that?" Lucy asked, pointing to the strange-looking device. Then she gasped. "Oh my God, you stole this car!"

"Just borrowed it. The owner is blissfully shopping at Marshall Fields. She'll never know."

"That is really scary," Lucy said. "That such a device even exists, and that our government employees steal cars."

"Government employees do a lot worse than steal cars, I'm afraid," he said as they exited the Mercedes. Unfortunately, he'd just found out the hard way what certain government employees were capable of.

Lucy grabbed the walker from the back seat, but she didn't use it. She walked beside him with a spring in her step, lithe and graceful. He led her to the car he'd arrived in, a silver Jaguar XJE. Since he'd been driving his personal wheels and not a "company car," he hadn't wanted to risk it being identified. Thus the switcheroo.

"Hmm, I liked this even better than the Mercedes," she commented as she put the walker in the trunk. "Is this one stolen, too?"

"No, this one's mine."

"I hadn't realized government employees earned enough money to afford a Jag."

"We don't. My government salary isn't my only source of income." He'd never imagined his cover business, the one he set up to satisfy friends and family, would turn so lucrative. He opened the passenger door for her. "You can ditch the disguise, now. We're safe."

"Thank God." She pulled off the wig. Her real hair pulled loose from its bun in the process, spilling over her shoulders in a rich chestnut cascade. He'd never found brown hair all that exciting before, but Lucy's was thick and luscious.

By the time he'd made it around to the driver's side, Lucy was out of her housecoat, which she'd thrown on over her white tailored blouse. Then she cursed. "I forgot my jeans."

"No, I put them in—" Then he stopped. He'd been so fascinated watching Lucy shimmy out of them, revealing a glimpse of her sensible white panties, that he *had* forgotten to bring the jeans along. "We'll get you some clothes, don't worry."

He had no business thinking about Lucy's panties, sensible or otherwise. He had a helluva problem here.

Finding the listening devices was disturbing enough. He'd been sure Lucy was exaggerating, that no one was following her or sneaking into her home. But she hadn't installed those listening devices herself.

In fact, once he'd examined the bug in her telephone, the list of suspects who could have planted it had shrunk to a handful. That bug was the latest technology, purchased from Russia. So new, in fact, that only his agency had access to it. Besides the Russians, of course. And he didn't think the Russians were involved in this.

Someone in his own organization had betrayed him, which meant his life and Lucy's weren't worth a used teabag unless he found out which agent was the Benedict Arnold—and neutralized him or her, fast.

Two

They drove in silence for a few minutes. Bryan took a circuitous route out of the city, darting on and off the freeway to be absolutely certain they weren't being followed. Then he headed north on Interstate 95 as a plan slowly formed.

"Are you okay?" he asked Lucy. She was awfully quiet. He'd expected her to be peppering him with questions about where they were going and what would happen next, questions to which he didn't have all the answers.

"I'm fine."

"I'm sorry I put you in danger."

"I knew what I was getting into when I signed on for this gig. You told me there would be some risk."

She didn't know the half of it. He'd never expected the risk to come from his own people. "You did great. I wish we could have finished the job, though."

"I did."

"Pardon me?"

"After I talked to you, I knew I wouldn't be returning to Alliance Trust. So I threw caution out the window. Before, I was careful to cover my tracks when I downloaded information. I figured that didn't matter anymore. So I just downloaded everything in sight. Practically the whole computer system. I can't believe how much that little memory stick holds."

"You downloaded everything?" he asked, hardly able to believe it.

"Everything I'll need. It will take some time to go through it all. Whoever was embezzling from the retirement funds was very sneaky. But I've got calendars, phone lists, log-on and log-off times, passwords, who attended what meeting when. Using a process of elimination, I can figure out who made the illicit withdrawals—I know I can."

"You won't have to. The agency has some of the best minds in the country—" He stopped. Until he knew who had betrayed him, he didn't dare turn this information over to anyone. One keystroke, and all of the evidence Lucy had risked her life for could be erased.

"I could do it," Lucy said. "I'm very good at puzzles. Maybe your organization has experts and high-tech equipment, but I know the people involved. I know how everything worked at that bank. No one is more qualified than me to analyze this data."

She might just be right. "What will you need?"

"A computer powerful enough to handle the amount of data involved. A quiet place to work. That's it."

The plan he'd been working on earlier became a bit firmer in his mind. It was kind of crazy. But he didn't know any other way to keep Lucy safe. He had access to any number of safe houses, but safe from whom? Everyone who was part of this mission knew those houses, too—Tarantula, Stungun, Orchid and his immediate supervisor, Siberia. His list of suspects. Four people whom, until an hour ago, he would have trusted with his life.

"I think I can accommodate you," he said.

"Okay, then." She settled back into her seat, looking satisfied. "Where are we going?"

Finally. He'd wondered when she would get around to asking that. "New York."

"Your home turf."

Bryan felt a prickle of apprehension. How did she know that?

"Your accent," she said before he had a chance to ask. "I went to school with a guy from New York. Long Island. You sound just like him."

Observant little thing, wasn't she? During his training, he'd learned to erase every trace of accent from his voice. His safety, and that of his wealthy family, depended on keeping every detail of his personal life separate from his life at the agency. It was like that for all the agents he worked with. They all used their code names, and they never revealed any personal information for any reason.

How had he let his guard down long enough that Lucy had figured out where he was from? Maybe he was slipping. Because of the intense pressure, a lot of agents didn't last long in the field.

"You work for the CIA?" she asked.

He used to. They'd recruited him in college, when he'd been studying business management with every intention of joining the family business, Elliott Publication Holdings. They said it was because of his straight As and his uncommon athleticism. He'd worked a lot of undercover.

Then a nameless, faceless person had recruited him to a newly formed investigative arm of Homeland Security, an agency so secret it didn't have a name. The agency had no central office, and it wasn't mentioned in the national budget. Basically it didn't exist.

Lying usually came easily to him. But for some reason he didn't want to lie straight-out to Lucy. He settled for a partial truth. "I work for Homeland Security."

"I didn't know Homeland Security had its own spies."

"Things are still evolving there."

"How does one become a spy?"

"Why, are you interested in joining up?"

"Maybe. Anything's better than what I was doing."

He'd only been kidding, but she was serious. "So why did you work at a bank if you didn't like it?"

She shrugged. "It was expected of me. And the money was pretty good. I'd been thinking about doing something else, though."

"Like what?"

"I dunno. Running away and joining the circus, maybe. I'd make a good lion tamer."

"You?" he blurted out, then wished he hadn't, given Lucy's reaction. He'd insulted her.

"Why couldn't I tame lions?"

"I'm sure you could. You could poke them with umbrellas."

"I think you're making fun of me. But you didn't think it was so funny when I had you on the floor. I almost gave you an impromptu tracheotomy with my trusty umbrella." She looked around the car. "Oh, we left it behind. I liked that umbrella."

"I'll buy you a new one," he said, feeling a bit sorry for her. Her life had been disrupted, and it would never be the same. He didn't think that fact had sunk into her head yet.

"We won't be going back, then," she said.

"Not in the foreseeable future."

"Good. If I'd had to spend one more night in that boring town house with its boring white walls, wearing those boring suits, I'd have slit my wrists."

She'd surprised him again. He'd done a considerable amount of research on Miss Lucy Miller. She came from a solid Kansas farming family, had attended the state university, got good grades. She'd been working at a job for which she was underqualified, but her employee reviews had come up glowing.

The only mystery about Lucy Miller was a period of about two years shortly after her college graduation, for which Bryan could not unearth much information. Her passport indicated she'd done some traveling abroad. The best he could figure, she'd been soaking up some culture before tying herself down to a serious career. She had an older brother who lived in Holland, so she might have been staying with him.

"My family will be worried," she said.

"You won't be able to contact them."

"Ever?" she asked in a small voice. "Am I going into the witness protection program?"

"Is that what you want?"

She sighed. "I could stand a new identity. I've always hated the name Lucy. But I want to pick the name."

"What would you pick?"

"Certainly not something as silly as Casanova—though I guess given the way you schmoozed Mrs. Pfluger, it fits. She's always been mean as a snake to me."

"Casanova wasn't my idea. You can call me Bryan." She would have learned his real name soon enough.

"And you can call me…Lindsay. Lindsay Morgan."

"Sounds very sophisticated. Does it have any significance? Do you know anyone named Lindsay? Or Morgan?"

"No. I've always liked the actress Lindsay Wagner. You know, the Bionic Woman. I catch it on late-night TV. And Morgan—I don't know. I pulled it out of thin air."

Exactly what Bryan wanted to hear. "Then Lindsay Morgan it is. Get used to it."

Oh, God, she thought, he was serious. She was really getting a new identity. A new life. A new job, a new home, maybe somewhere exciting like New York. She knew she should be terrified. Ruthless criminals with ties to international terrorism had broken into her home and planted bugs. They might even now be searching for her, intending to kill her.

But she could feel nothing but anticipation.

She wished her parents didn't have to worry, though. She wanted to ask Bryan if she would ever see them again. But she had a feeling he really didn't know the answer to that question. Something was troubling him. She got the feeling he was on shaky ground, that the turn this investigation had taken had thrown him for a loop.

He hadn't believed her when she'd told him she was being followed. He'd only come to her town house because she'd threatened to disappear with all the data.

He'd been very surprised to discover she was right, that the operation was blown to bits.

Did he suspect she was the one who'd blown it?

"I didn't give myself away," she said abruptly, wanting to clear this up right now. "I was extremely careful. Until today I did the downloading only five or ten minutes at a time, always when I was alone in my office, the door closed. I never said anything to anyone. Ever. And no one had access to the memory stick. I kept it in my bra."

He looked over at her. "Really? Is it there now?"

"Yes."

The car swerved slightly, and not for any apparent reason. Lucy wondered if something as innocent as mentioning her bra had startled Bryan. But how could it? The guy was a spy—he'd probably seen things unimaginable to normal people. Surely the mention of women's underwear wouldn't faze him.

Especially *her* underwear, which was about as boring as underwear could get.

It had been a very long time since anything she said or did had any effect on the opposite sex. She had buried that flirtatious, reckless girl under a frumpy suit, thick glasses and mousy hair, and she'd done it for a reason, she reminded herself.

So Bryan had probably been avoiding a bump in the road.

They drove for almost five hours, but the days were long in July, so it was still daylight when they hit New York. Lucy had been to the city many times, but it had been a while, and she'd forgotten how much she loved it. New York had an energy unlike any other city in the universe. Even if she'd had her eyes closed, she'd have known she was here. The traffic noise and exhaust fumes were peculiar only to this place.

"Are we staying in Manhattan?" she asked.

"Yes."

"Are you putting me up in a hotel?"

"No. I don't want to go anyplace where ID is required until we get your new name officially established."

"A safe house, then?"

"The safest."

He flashed her a brief smile, and it was the first time she'd seen him looking anything but grim since they'd met. That smile did things to her insides. No wonder cranky Mrs. Pfluger had become so cooperative. If Bryan had taken ten more minutes, the older woman probably would have dropped her own pants. Jeez, Lucy couldn't believe she'd taken off her jeans in front of a strange man. But she'd been just panicked enough not to care.

They'd crossed over to Manhattan via the Lincoln Tunnel, and in midtown they were surrounded by skyscrapers, buses, cars, taxis and pedestrians. People were everywhere. And such interesting people! All colors, shapes and sizes. Some were elegantly dressed—theatergoers on their way to catch the curtain perhaps. Some in bedraggled business attire, waving down taxis, looked like they were just getting off from a long day at the office. And of course there were the ubiquitous colorful characters—hot-dog vendors, shady men selling designer-watch knock-offs and bootleg DVDs, and your garden-variety vagrants.

She'd forgotten how much she loved this city, though it held some painful reminders, as well. Normally she didn't allow herself to think about her last time here, when she'd made a headlong dash home, crying the entire way. But now she did, and she found the pain wasn't so sharp anymore. She felt more sad and wistful than anything.

She'd healed during the past two years. She'd needed the downtime, the safe haven her job at the bank had provided. But she was ready to move on now—older and wiser. She was actually grateful to the embezzler, whoever he or she was, for shaking her out of her boring, complacent life, or she might have remained there indefinitely, afraid to live again.

She was living now, that was for sure. Riding up Tenth Avenue in a Jaguar with a spy. Not your everyday occurrence.

Lucy cracked open her window, and the wonderful city smells assailed her. She got a whiff of some exotic food—garlic, tarragon, curry—and her stomach rumbled. It occurred to her she hadn't eaten since breakfast, and even then she'd barely managed to choke down some yogurt. She'd been too nervous about her situation.

"I'm starving," she said. "Any chance this safe house will have food in the fridge? Or maybe we can order in Chinese?" she asked hopefully.

"Don't worry, I'll feed you."

They were driving through the Upper West Side now, the street lined with posh shops, trendy restaurants and bodegas, and residential high-rises where the beautiful people lived. Most of her time in New York had been spent around here, near Cruz's apartment.

They passed a restaurant called Une Nuit—"One Night" in French. Though it was early by Manhattan standards, a line of trendily dressed hopefuls was already forming at the door.

"I read about that place," she said, nodding toward it. "In *People* magazine, I think. Or maybe *The Buzz*. Some movie star had a birthday party there or something."

"It was one of the Hilton sisters."

"Oh, so you keep up with the gossip? How does a spy have time to read *The Buzz?*"

"Actually, I didn't read about it. I was there."

"No kidding? You know the Hilton sisters?" Lucy had always been starstruck. She'd been addicted to celebrity magazines since junior high and had fantasized about someday being one of the beautiful people—or at least hanging out with them.

She'd learned the hard way that the celebrity scene wasn't all parties and glamour. In fact, beneath all the glitz, it could get pretty rotten. But even after her unhappy brush with that life, she hadn't lost her fascination with it.

Bryan didn't answer, but he pulled his car around a corner and into an underground garage, inserting a pass card to gain entrance.

"Um, we're not actually stopping to eat, are we?" Lucy asked, looking down at her orange polyester pants. "I mean, I'd love to go to that restaurant someday, but they wouldn't let me in the door dressed like this."

He grinned. "I could get you in. But, no, we're not going there right now. This is actually your safe house." He pulled into a reserved parking space and cut the engine.

"Seems a funny place for a safe house," she commented. "I thought we'd be a little more…isolated."

"A safe house can be anywhere, so long as no one

knows about it." He led her through a door that was marked Entrance Une Nuit. But once inside a small, featureless foyer, they didn't follow the signs to the restaurant. They boarded a rickety-looking elevator. Bryan pushed a button that had no floor number on it.

"Password, please," came a computerized voice.

"Enchilada coffee," Bryan replied. The elevator started up.

The amazement on Lucy's expressive face gave Bryan a rush of pleasure, and he had to admit that, despite the gravity of his situation, he was enjoying Lucy's reactions. He'd expected her to be a basket case, a perpetually panicked paranoid. But she'd risen to the occasion, showing a presence of mind few civilians possessed.

"How James Bond," Lucy said. "The elevator is password protected?"

"With the latest voice-recognition software. No one gets into this loft but me—and my guests, of course."

"So this is where you *live?*"

"Yeah. You have a problem with that?"

"No, but it seems a little odd, that's all. I didn't think spies normally brought witnesses in protective custody to their homes."

"They don't. This is a special occasion."

"Why? Surely this case isn't a particularly big or significant one. You must have dozens, *hundreds* of people attempting to funnel funds to terrorists."

He debated how much to tell her. But he decided she could handle the truth. He wanted her to understand she could trust no one but him. "I have strong reason to believe I've been betrayed by my own people—which means there's not a safe house in our system that's truly safe. This is the one place I could think of where no one could possibly find you."

"You mean, the people you work with—the other spies—don't know where you live?"

"They don't even know my name. To the others in my cell, and even to my boss, I'm Casanova."

"Wow."

The elevator doors opened, and Bryan led Lucy into his private living space. A couple of years ago, he'd bought the entire building where Une Nuit was located. He'd renovated and expanded the dining area, used the second floor for offices and storage, and had the top two floors converted to living space.

He'd spared no expense—he hadn't had to. Though he had some family money, and he was well paid as a top-echelon government agent, this was the home that Une Nuit had built. The restaurant, which he'd originally opened as a cover so that not even his closest friends and family would know of his true vocation, had become unexpectedly popular—and lucrative.

The apartment's floor plan wasn't completely open, but a few interior walls had been placed at odd angles so the place didn't feel like a box. The foyer opened up on one side to an enormous, modern kitchen he'd designed himself, with the latest in brushed-steel appliances. The kitchen was open to the living room, which faced a row of tall windows looking out onto Columbus Avenue. The floor was the original warehouse planking, sanded and polished to a high sheen. Some walls he had left as natural brick, while he'd had others plastered and painted a pristine white.

The furnishings were ultramodern, comfortable but sparse. He did his entertaining in the restaurant, so he didn't need lots of chairs or sofas. Original art adorned the space, but again, not too much—a small abstract painting here, a funky sculpture there. Things he'd seen, wanted, picked up. Mostly from starving artists getting their starts, although a few pieces might be worth some serious money by now.

"I love this place!" Lucy whirled around, trying to take it all in. "You live here? You actually live here?"

"When I'm home, which lately hasn't been all that often."

"How long will I be staying here? Not that I'm complaining, just trying to prepare myself. Will you want me to testify at a trial? Will I have to stay indoors all the time, or can I go out?"

He smiled at her exuberance, which radiated from her every pore. He'd thought her plain when he first saw her, but he could see that wasn't true, even in those horrible orange pants. She had an infectious smile and bright, lively eyes in a shade of pale blue he'd seldom seen.

"I won't keep you locked up like a prisoner," he said. "We'll be able to venture out some. I don't imagine you'll run into anyone you know this far from home." As for his family, there was no way to avoid them. He would have to find a way to explain her sudden presence in his life.

"Um, actually, that's not true," she said. "I lived here for a while."

"What?" This was news to him. The exhaustive background check he'd done on her hadn't mentioned any residences in New York. "That's impossible." But then he remembered those two years when she'd disappeared from the system.

"Have you ever heard of a band called In Tight?" she asked.

"Sure. They're hot right now. In fact, didn't they play the Super Bowl half-time this year?"

She nodded. "I used to work for them."

Now it was Bryan's turn to be shocked. "You? Working for a rock band?"

"I answered an ad on the Internet, and I got a job working on In Tight's finances—you know, helping to manage the money when they did concert tours, stuff like that."

Bryan had a hard time picturing Lucy Miller hanging out with wild-haired musicians. Was it possible she was pulling his leg? Was Lucy Miller a pathological liar?

"I did a background check on you," he said. "There was nothing about—"

"They paid me off the books. They weren't as famous then. They gave me a place to live, too, so you wouldn't have found an apartment under my name. I'm just telling you this so you'll know that I might run into people who would recognize me."

"We'll just have to make sure that doesn't happen." He studied her from head to toe, thinking how she could be made to look different—different hair, different eyes. "How would you feel about a makeover?"

He was worried that he'd insulted her, but instead she brightened. "Oh, I'd love one. Can I be a blonde? I think Lindsay Morgan would be a blonde."

"If you like. My cousin Scarlet is the assistant fashion editor at *Charisma* magazine. She can bring over a truckload of clothes and cosmetics, hair stuff. Do you need the glasses?"

"Only if I don't want to run into walls."

"We'll get you some contacts. Maybe green ones, though it's a shame to cover up those pretty blue eyes."

She looked away, embarrassed. "Don't tease me. My eyes are a very ordinary shade of blue—almost gray. Boring."

"I don't find them boring at all."

She peeked up at him. "You're serious."

Maybe he shouldn't have said anything. He didn't want Lucy feeling threatened, since she was forced to shack up with him. "Don't worry, I'm not going to hit on you. But you do have pretty eyes."

"Hit on me. Right. So when is the magical transformation going to take place?"

"How about after dinner?"

Bryan showed Lucy to the guest room, which had a private bath. "Where do you sleep?" she asked.

"My room's upstairs, along with a study. I'll show you later. My computer's up there, and if you're serious about deciphering the data you brought from the bank, you'll be spending a lot of time at the keyboard."

"Absolutely."

"I'll leave you to freshen up, then, while I do something about dinner."

"Okay. Do you have a robe or something I can wear until your cousin brings me some clothes? I don't really want to put Mrs. Pfluger's polyester pants back on after my shower. In fact, I'd like to burn them."

"I'll bring you something."

Bryan didn't actually have a robe, but he found her a pair of pajamas still in the package, a gift from his gram. Every year she gave him pajamas, and he'd never had the nerve to tell her he didn't wear them.

When he returned to Lucy's room, the shower was

running, the bathroom door open a crack. He felt a less-than-admirable urge to peek inside the bath and see what she looked like without clothes. Ever since she'd fallen on top of him, his imagination had been running wild.

He didn't, then wondered why he was being so noble. He was a spy, used to peering at other people's secrets. He set the pajamas on the bed and then went to see about dinner. A quick call downstairs to the restaurant took care of that. Then he had to deal with Scarlet.

"You know I love a makeover challenge," Scarlet said, warming to the idea right away. "John's away on business, so my evening's free. I'll stop by the office, grab everything I need and be there in an hour or so."

"Are you guys getting married?"

"The wedding's not till next year, and if you didn't travel so much for the restaurant, you would know these things. Honestly, don't they grow decent spices in America?"

Hmm. Maybe his standard excuse for his frequent absences—that he was seeking exotic spices—was growing a little thin. "I have to keep up with the latest," he said blandly.

"So where'd you find this girl, anyway? What's the story? Normally the girls I've seen you with don't need any help in the clothes or cosmetics department."

"Oh, she's not my—" He stopped. How was he going to explain Lucy's presence to Scarlet, and to the rest of his family? She could be under his protection for months. He couldn't keep her under wraps all that time. "She's not my usual type, true," he continued smoothly. "But Lindsay's special. Frankly, I think she's perfect just the way she is. She's a country girl, you know, the all-natural look. But she's the one who wants a makeover. She wants to fit in better in New York."

"I'll be happy to help Lindsay any way I can," Scarlet said, and Bryan read between the lines. She was going to pump Lucy for every shred of information she could get about Bryan's new romance. He'd better go warn Lucy that she'd just become his girlfriend.

Three

Lucy couldn't believe what she'd just overheard. She hadn't meant to eavesdrop. But as she wandered into the kitchen fresh from her shower, she couldn't help but hear Bryan talking to his cousin. And he'd passed her off as his new girlfriend.

Bryan turned, saw her and realized she'd heard. "Uh, yeah. Guess we need to talk about this. I'm sorry, but I don't know any other way to explain what you're doing here. My family doesn't know I'm a government agent. No one knows. And they can't know. I have to keep those two parts of my life completely separate, for the welfare of everyone concerned. You understand that, right?"

"Yes. But—"

"You've already proved you can be cool under pressure. When Scarlet gets here, just follow my lead. You're okay with this, right?"

Oh, she was more than okay. The idea excited her. But there was a big problem. "Sure, I can deal with it, but who on earth is going to believe I'm your girlfriend?"

"Why wouldn't they?"

"Because I'm just a mousy little banker from D.C. and you're a…a…"

"I own a restaurant. That's all anyone knows." The phone rang and he picked it up. It didn't escape Lucy's attention that he didn't argue about her self-assessment. Apparently he agreed with her description of "mousy."

"Okay, thanks." He hung up and turned back to Lucy. "That's our dinner. I'll be right back."

While he was gone, Lucy tried to wrap her mind around the idea that she was going to be posing as Bryan's girlfriend. Once upon a time she'd thought of herself as quite the hot chick. After all, she'd caught the eye of Cruz Tabor, drummer for In Tight, one of the hottest men in the country if the tabloids could be believed. She'd told herself when she took the job with In Tight that she wouldn't behave like a groupie, that just being around the band was excitement enough for her.

Then Cruz had started flirting with her, and she was a goner. She'd believed every lie the bastard had told her. He'd said she was gorgeous, sexy, hot. He'd taken her on tour, letting her travel in first class with the band, buying her expensive presents.

But then she'd discovered he said all those things, did all those things, with every woman he slept with. And there were lots and lots of them. She'd been so naive, such a dumb bunny, to think she was anything special.

This was way different, though, she reminded herself. She *wasn't* a hot chick, and she wasn't deluding herself into believing she was. So how would anyone else believe she'd caught Bryan's eye? Bryan was pretty hot himself. He could have any woman he wanted.

He knew the Hilton sisters. His trendy restaurant drew celebrities all the time. Did he sleep with any of them? How was she supposed to compete with that?

She found some dishes in the cabinets and set two place settings at the polished-granite bar. A few minutes later, the most wonderful aroma invaded her nose, followed by Bryan stepping off the elevator with two huge white bags.

Lucy's stomach rumbled again. "What *is* that?"

"Shrimp and vegetable stir-fry Polonnaise. It's not too spicy, and you can pick out anything you don't like."

"Stir-fry with a French sauce?"

"Right. That's what Une Nuit is all about—Asian and French fusion dishes." He set the bags on the counter, then gave her a quick once-over. She was wearing his pajama top with nothing on underneath. It was modest enough, covering all the important bits and hanging almost to her knees, so in deference to the fact it was summer in New York, she hadn't bothered with the bottoms.

Now she wished she had. She felt suddenly vulnerable with her bare legs and a breeze from the air conditioner stirring around her private parts.

"Nice look," he said with a wink. Then he turned and started unpacking the bags, stacking a mound of food on each plate and not even noticing that the hair on her forearms stood on end and her skin was flushed with awareness.

Oh, grow up, she scolded herself. He'd probably seen

a hundred women wearing a lot less than a shapeless pajama top adorned with—yes, scenes from France.

He selected a bottle of chilled white wine from a climate-controlled wine safe as big as a refrigerator. "You like wine?"

"I don't— Why, yes, I do." She'd been about to say she didn't drink. Alcohol was one of the things she'd given up when she'd made the decision to change her life, grow up, live like a conscientious adult instead of a wild, irresponsible teenager.

But after the day she'd had, a nice glass of Chardonnay sounded really nice. And it wasn't as if she'd ever been an excessive drinker. But copious alcohol consumption by the people around her had been a big part of the life she'd left behind.

Bryan filled two crystal glasses and handed her one. "A toast. To your new life as Lindsay Morgan."

"To Lindsay." She clinked her glass with his and took a sip of the crisp, dry wine. This whole thing was so surreal.

She hopped up on a bar stool and dived into the food, which was absolutely the most incredible meal she'd ever eaten. "Oh, my God, this is so good. No wonder your restaurant is so successful. Did you start it, or buy it as an ongoing concern?"

"It was a moderately profitable French bistro when I bought it. Merging French with Asian started out as a joke, really, one night when the manager, the chef and I had a little too much to drink. Then I thought, why not? We all started experimenting in the kitchen, adding one thing and then another to the menu, and it just exploded in popularity."

"I can see why." Her taste buds were cheering over

the subtle blend of exotic spices and the delicate textures, while the beautiful blend of colors and shapes and aromas engaged her other senses. She ate it all and didn't regret it a bit, even when she was stuffed. If Bryan was going to feed her like this every day, she was going to have to use the home gym she'd seen tucked away in another bedroom.

When they finished, Lucy hand washed the dishes and put them away—no sense running the dishwasher for two people. A buzzer alerted them to Scarlet's arrival, and Bryan went down to greet her and help her carry up her things.

Lucy was nervous about meeting Bryan's cousin. She hadn't had to deal with a boyfriend's family since high school. She tried to tell herself it didn't matter whether Scarlet liked her. Bryan wasn't her real boyfriend, and this situation was temporary. When they caught the embezzler, she would start a new life away from here and she'd probably never lay eyes on Bryan or Scarlet again.

But it did matter. She still wanted Scarlet to like her. But she figured she would be found sadly lacking. The woman was an assistant fashion editor for one of the hottest women's magazines in the country, after all. Scarlet was used to dressing supermodels and movie stars, not frumpy little bankers wearing oversize men's pajamas.

The elevator opened, and Bryan returned carrying an enormous armload of clothing. Following him was one of the most beautiful, exotic creatures Lucy had ever seen. She was almost as tall as Bryan, reed slim, with a gorgeous head of light-auburn hair that fell in abundant, bright waves around her shoulders and down her back. She wore a bright-green, gauzy off-the-shoulder shirt and snug pants in a coordinating print, all of which set off her pale-green eyes—eyes that zeroed in on Lucy and missed nothing.

"So you're my victim," she said cheerfully, dropping her own armload of clothing, a shopping bag and a cosmetic case the size of an industrial tool chest. She came forward, hand outstretched. "Hi, I'm Scarlet. You must be Lindsay."

Lucy uttered some pleasantry, but inside she was trembling. What had she gotten herself into? She was living a lie, starting right now. What if she couldn't pull this off? Bryan had been very clear about how important it was to keep his secret agent life separate from his family, and she wouldn't be able to live with herself if she messed that up for him.

"Stand up," Scarlet said. "Let's see what we have to work with."

Bryan leaned one elbow on the bar and watched, obviously interested in the proceedings, and Lucy felt her face heating again. This was going to be embarrassing enough without *him* watching, seeing her every physical flaw pointed out.

Scarlet apparently sensed Lucy's unease, because she turned to her cousin. "Don't you have something to do? A restaurant to run? Stash was complaining to me that you're piling too much work on him with all your gallivanting around Europe and Asia."

"I want to see what you're going to do with her."

"No," she said firmly. "Lindsay's makeover is about her, not your fantasies of the perfect woman. Now go away. And stay gone at least until midnight."

Bryan grumbled, but he turned and headed for the elevator. Then he abruptly changed direction and walked up to Lucy. "Have fun, okay? I'll see you in a while." And then he touched her cheek, gently angling her face toward him, and kissed her lightly on the mouth.

The kiss lasted maybe half a second, but it electrified everything inside Lucy from her toes to her scalp, and she had to grip the back of the bar stool she'd just vacated to keep from keeling over.

Oh, Lord, she was in trouble. She knew deep down that it was all an act, that Bryan had been working undercover for years and that the ruse of a girlfriend came as easily as breathing to him. But it was all new to her. The casual possessiveness he'd treated her to had felt awfully damn real.

Scarlet, apparently oblivious to the tidal wave of feelings coursing through Lucy, was testing the weight and texture of Lucy's still-damp hair.

"You've got great hair," she said. "Thick and healthy. It'll do just about anything you want. I assume you'll want to keep most of the length, but we can do some layers—"

"No. I want it short. I want it to look as different as possible. And blond."

"You want highlights?"

"Oh, no. I want to be radically blond."

Scarlet grinned. "I'm so glad you said that. I was prepared to be cautious, but if you'll trust me—let me go crazy on you—you'll be ready for a *Charisma* cover shoot when I'm done."

Lucy laughed self-consciously. "Well, I hardly think that."

"Why not? You've got excellent bone structure, regular features, good teeth. The glasses, though, have got to go."

"I want contacts," she said, remembering Bryan's instructions. "I want green eyes. Bright green. But I'm afraid there's not much you can do about my figure."

"Hey, most of our models have even less in the chest department than you do. You'd be surprised what good foundation garments can do. You're slender, which means the clothes will fit you. Help me carry all this stuff into the bedroom and we can get started."

"I'm staying—" Lucy almost blew it in the first five minutes. If she was Bryan's girlfriend, she wouldn't be in the guest room; she would be sharing the master bedroom with him. "I'll be staying here for quite awhile, I guess, and I don't have any clothes at all. I'll need everything." There. She congratulated herself on a skillful recovery.

"What happened to your clothes?" Scarlet wanted to know, obviously sensing a juicy story. "And don't worry, nothing you could say would shock me. My twin sister is marrying a rock star."

"Really? Which one?" Please, dear God, don't let it be anyone she knew, anyone with In Tight.

"Zeke Woodlow."

Lucy was infinitely relieved—until she put it all together. She'd read about Zeke's engagement in *The Buzz*. "Your sister is Summer Elliott. You're the Elliott family, the ones who *own* all those magazines." One of the richest families on the Eastern Seaboard.

Scarlet looked startled. "You didn't know that?"

Maybe she'd just better shut up. "I didn't know Bryan was one of *the* Elliotts. I'm a little slow—just putting it together now. We haven't been dating for long," she added, hoping that would explain away her cluelessness. "As for my clothes, I, uh, burned them. I need a fresh start."

"Burned them? Where?"

Belatedly Lucy remembered you couldn't burn anything in New York—it was against the law.

"Back home."

"Where's home?"

"Kansas. On a farm." That much, at least, was true. She'd grown up in a small, conservative Kansas farming town, and her parents were still there.

"What was Bryan doing in Kansas? I thought he was in Europe."

"Oh, he was. We met in Paris."

"Then you went home to the farm, burned your clothes and came back here? Naked?"

Lucy smiled as if this wasn't the most ridiculous story anyone had ever tried to pass off as the truth. "Right."

"Girlfriend, I like your style."

Bryan was still trying to recover his equilibrium as he headed down to the restaurant. He'd realized he was going to have to make it look good if his family was ever going to believe Lucy was his girlfriend. He'd never had a serious relationship before. Well, he'd tried once, but he'd quickly found out that women didn't like it when he disappeared for weeks at a time. He'd decided that as long as he was in the spy business, it wasn't fair to any woman to try to have a relationship. Not only would they have to put up with frequent absences, but there was always the chance he wouldn't come home.

If that ever happened, the poor woman would probably never find out his fate.

So he dated casually. He occasionally slept with a woman if she was hot, willing and understood the ground rules. He'd seldom brought a woman into his loft, and he'd certainly never installed one as a live-in mistress. For his family to buy "Lindsay's" sudden presence in his life, he was going to have to claim he was utterly smitten. And that meant acting the adoring boyfriend, with public displays of affection, longing glances, the whole nine yards.

He probably should have prepared Lucy better for the role she was playing. They hadn't even gone over a cover story—where Lucy was from, where they'd met.

Oh, well, Lucy was smart enough to wing it. As long as she reported back to him any details she'd given Scarlet, so they could keep the story consistent, it would be okay.

As for that kiss, Lucy had looked like the proverbial deer in the headlights when he'd swooped in for the light smooch. But he was the one who'd been surprised. Her lips had been soft and warm, and her vulnerability had somehow transmitted itself straight from her soul to his, all in the half second of contact between their mouths.

It had been the merest brushing of lips, so innocent, yet it had shaken him to his shoes. No kiss had ever done that.

He'd mostly composed himself by the time he entered the restaurant kitchen, but the memory of the kiss remained in the back of his mind.

"Hey, boss, you're back!" one of the sous-chefs greeted him.

"*Monsieur* Bryan!" called out another. "Hey, those Florentine eggrolls are going like hotcakes."

The head chef, Kim Chin, who ran the kitchen like a marine bootcamp, looked up from his sauté pan and grunted a greeting. "'Bout time."

All right, so he'd been neglecting his business lately. No one said it was easy working two jobs, and the

Alliance Trust case had been occupying every waking hour these days. While Lucy had worked it from her end, Bryan had been tracking down the people receiving the embezzled funds, working with two French agents to prevent any of the illicit funds from reaching terrorists in Iraq while not tipping off the bad guys on the American side. Not until he had them all rounded up could he assemble the evidence needed to put them away for a good long time.

"Where's Stash?" he asked Kim.

"Out schmoozing the beautiful people, of course, the worthless Frenchie." Which was pretty funny, since Stash practically lived at the restaurant, keeping everything running, paying the bills, meeting payroll, handling all the hundreds of details that kept Une Nuit at the top of everyone's list.

"Bryan, you're back!" Stash greeted him with a hearty hug and a double air-kiss. Stash Martin was an energetic Frenchman in his thirties. With equal parts stubbornness and optimism, he was the perfect manager for an often absent owner. "What keeps you away for so long, eh?" he asked with a French accent. "The place could have been turned into a hot-dog stand while you were gone."

Bryan had prepared a long, shaggy-dog story about his exploits in Europe. Instead he said, "I met someone." He had to set up Lucy's cover story, he reasoned. Lying came easily to him, given the number of years he'd worked undercover. But the scary thing was, he didn't have to manufacture the edge in his voice when he talked about Lucy. What had started as a fairly routine job had turned into something exciting and challenging—and for all the wrong reasons.

* * *

Lucy stared at herself in the mirror, then stared some more. Scarlet hadn't allowed her to watch the transformation, so her own image was a complete surprise. No, a shock. Her mother wouldn't recognize her—which was the point, of course.

Her brown hair lay in piles on the floor. Scarlet had cut it to chin length, dyed it to a pale blond, then blow-dried it straight so that it fell in a shimmering fringe that bounced with her every move. Her eyebrows had been plucked and reshaped, and the artfully applied cosmetics had sculpted her face and redefined the shape of her mouth. She now had cheekbones.

Then there were the clothes. After sorting through the piles and piles of glamorous outfits, Scarlet had decided that Lucy needed a look, and had chosen an array of clingy knits in a palette of soft colors—mossy green, plum, cantaloupe, tawny gold. The outfit she wore now was a pair of green low-rider pants and a cropped tank top that clung to all her curves. A second shirt in a paler green, with a front zipper and short sleeves, went over the tank. Wedge-heeled sandals and bold jewelry completed the look.

The most amazing thing, though, was the fact that she had cleavage. Scarlet had found her a really clever push-up bra that made her A cups look like Cs.

Lucy kept putting her glasses on to look at herself from far away, then taking them off and peering at her face from close up. She just couldn't believe it. She *did* look like someone who could be Bryan Elliott's girl-friend. Someone who belonged in New York. When she'd lived here before, she'd never felt quite at home, never really shed her Kansas persona.

"This is just amazing," she said for about the third time.

"The models you see in magazines don't have anything we don't have," Scarlet said. "Hairstylists, makeup artists, good lighting and a skilled photographer can turn the plainest-looking woman into a knock-out."

Lucy was convinced. But she wasn't sure the Lucy Miller on the inside matched the one on the outside. Beautiful women—like Scarlet—had an inner confidence, a way of moving and talking that Lucy lacked.

"What if I can't carry it off?" she asked in a small voice.

"You'll manage. Listen, I can't imagine Bryan hooking up with a woman who isn't really, really special. He saw something in you, something inside. Just remember that, and you'll be fine."

Oh, yeah. What Scarlet didn't know was that Bryan didn't pick her at all. She'd dropped into his lap, and now he was stuck with her.

"So are you close to Bryan?" Lucy asked, figuring this was a golden opportunity to find out more about her supposed boyfriend.

"All the Elliott cousins are close. Here, stand up on the bed and let me shorten those pants. You're as slim as a model, but not quite as tall as one."

"Do most of you work for the magazines?" Lucy asked, trying not to think about the fact she was standing on Bryan's bed, trying not to think of him sleeping there. Or doing something else.

"We all work for Elliott Publication Holdings in one capacity or another. Except Bryan. He's the only one to escape that fate."

"Why is that, do you think?"

"Oh, he had other ideas from the time he was young. His heart problem kept him somewhat separated from the rest of us, I think. Until he had his operation, he couldn't run and play with us, and we were an extremely active bunch. Turn."

Lucy obediently turned, but her mind was reeling. Heart problem? Bryan?

"By the time they fixed his heart, his interest in food and cooking had already developed. Then he got into sports, bigtime—had to outdo his brother and all his cousins, as if he was making up for lost time. The magazines just didn't hold any appeal for him, I guess. Oh, he studied finance in school with some vague notion of going to work for the company, but that didn't last long. He wanted to do his own thing. He may have been the smartest one in the bunch."

"Why would you say that? Working for *Charisma* must be like a dream."

"Ordinarily, yes. But with the competition going on— Oh, Bryan probably didn't tell you about that, and why would he?"

Lucy was intrigued. "What competition? Tell me."

"My grandfather has decided to retire and make one of his children the CEO of the corporation. Each is currently head of one of the magazines—*Pulse, Snap, The Buzz* and *Charisma.* So the one whose magazine shows the biggest profit growth by the end of the year wins the top spot. Needless to say, everyone is at each other's throats. My boss, Aunt Fin, practically lives at the magazine, she's so obsessed with winning. And Uncle Michael— Well, his wife, my Aunt Karen, is recovering from breast cancer and he should be focusing on that, not worrying about a stupid contest."

Scarlet had gotten a bit worked up, and she stopped suddenly. "I'm sorry. Bryan would skewer me like a shish-kebab if he knew I was airing family laundry to his new girl."

"I won't say anything," Lucy assured her.

Lucy glanced at her new watch—a big, copper-colored bracelet thing—and was surprised to see it was after 1 a.m. Bryan wasn't home yet. What was he doing, she wondered. He obviously wasn't anxious to get back to her. It was probably a relief to be free of her for a while.

"Well, I hate to undo your hard work, but I think I'll take off all this makeup and turn in," Lucy said. "It's been a long day. Thank you so much, Scarlet. It was really nice of you to spend your evening this way."

"My pleasure, believe me. It was nice to get away from family and work pressure for a while." The two women embraced, and Lucy felt a rush of warmth and gratitude to Scarlet. She hadn't had any close girlfriends the last couple of years since moving to D.C. A few women at work had invited her occasionally to join them for dinner or drinks or a movie, but she'd kept her distance. She'd told herself it was because she wanted to keep her focus on work and not get distracted until her career was better established. But she could see now she'd been punishing herself. Having fun had gotten her into a lot of trouble. Therefore, fun was bad and it had to be eliminated from her life.

She imagined Scarlet already had a full complement of friends, though. Anyway, Lucy probably wouldn't have time for socializing. She had to go through all the data she'd downloaded from the bank and figure out who the embezzler was.

She helped Scarlet pack up her things and walked her

to the elevator. "I'd walk you down and help you carry all this, but I don't know how to get back in."

Scarlet rolled her eyes. "Bryan's silly elevator. He does have some pretty valuable artwork he doesn't want stolen, but he so overdid it with the security."

Maybe, but Lucy was grateful for it. They said goodbye. Then Lucy headed back up to the loft's upper level, which housed the master suite and Bryan's study. She wanted to move all of her things back down to her own bedroom before Bryan returned.

No such luck. She heard the elevator as she was heading down the stairs with an armload of clothing, her new wardrobe.

"Lucy?" he called out as he strode into the living room. "Oh, there you are. It took longer than I thought to go through the—" He stopped midstride and stared at her. "What have you done to your hair?"

"You…you don't like it?" Lucy squeaked. Scarlet had pointed out that men liked long hair, and Bryan might not be too keen on the short 'do. Her hair barely skimmed her jawline. Lucy had hesitated only briefly. The point was to look different, not to please Bryan.

But now she realized how badly she wanted him to like the new Lucy. Or rather, Lindsay.

"You just look so— Come down here. Put those clothes down and let me have a look at you."

Lucy did as asked, laying the beautiful new clothes on a chair and standing there, feeling enormously self-conscious as Bryan looked her up and down, then walked behind her and all around her, his expression unreadable.

He came closer and reached toward her face. She tried not to react as he removed her glasses and studied her features.

"Scarlet gave me the name of an optometrist who can fit me with green contacts. I can do that tomorrow."

"Okay." He didn't give her back the glasses. Instead, he stuck them in his shirt pocket.

"Well?" she said impatiently. "Will I do? Or do I just look ridiculous?" Maybe she was a sow's ear that couldn't pass muster as a silk purse.

A smile spread slowly across Bryan's face, which was a bit blurry to her. "Oh, you'll do, all right. Lucy, you look like a movie star." His gaze on her was like a heat lamp. Or maybe the heat was coming from inside her. She couldn't see him all that well, after all. She was probably imagining the blatant interest in the way he looked at her.

Suddenly, all she could think about was the way he'd kissed her earlier, so casually, and how she'd almost melted on the spot. It was all a game to him, but she wasn't used to being deceptive.

"Don't you think you should start calling me Lindsay all the time?" she said, sounding testy even to her own ears. "And if you're going to kiss me like you did, at least give me a little warning."

"We're supposed to be besotted with each other, so you can expect me to kiss you just about any time."

"O-okay."

"You don't sound too sure." He grasped her upper arms with both hands and looked deeply into her eyes. "Do you think you can pull this off? If not, we'll have to think of something else. My family can't suspect the truth. That would be a disaster."

Lucy was disturbed by the idea that he might change his mind, take her somewhere else, dump her in some hotel or something. In a very short time, she'd accustomed herself to the idea that she would be posing as Bryan's live-in lover.

"I can pull it off," she said. "But if we could rehearse—I mean, get our stories worked out, so I could, you know, know what to expect—"

He was watching her mouth. She stopped self-consciously. "Have I smeared my lipstick?"

"No, sweetheart, you look perfect. I was just thinking that we can't have you looking like a startled cat every time I touch you or kiss you. So you're right, of course. We need to rehearse." And with that, he slanted his mouth against hers and kissed her as if he meant it.

Four

Lucy tasted like wild cherries. Maybe it was her lipstick, or maybe it was just how Lucy Miller tasted, but what Bryan had intended as a friendly, you-don't-have-to-be-afraid-of-me kiss had turned into something much more.

Before he knew what was happening, Lucy's arms had snaked around his neck, and she was kissing him back in a way that told him *fear* wasn't in her vocabulary. She kissed as though she was born to it. Clearly she wasn't the inexperienced virginal miss he'd pegged her for.

Or maybe he'd awakened some innate talent she had. He liked that idea better. He didn't want to think about Lucy kissing other men, sleeping with other men.

Not that he would be sleeping with her. That would be taking their ruse a bit far. But kissing—for the sake of her cover story—was okay.

It was more than okay. He groaned as he buried his

hands in her newly shortened locks. Her hair felt like the softest silk, and he found he didn't really miss all that long, heavy hair. He liked the way the short ends tickled his hands and arms.

He stopped just short of pulling her hips against his and letting her know just exactly how okay her kiss was. But he did invade her mouth with his tongue, deepening the kiss, breathing in the heady scent of cosmetics and shampoo and new clothes that clung to her.

He'd never known new clothes could smell so sexy.

She pulled away suddenly, staring at him with wide, startled eyes. "What are you doing?"

That was a very good question. He casually pulled his hands out of her hair. "I thought we were rehearsing. Getting comfortable with each other."

"Well…okay, I got it. That's enough practice."

He couldn't help grinning. "You sure?"

"Yes, quite sure."

She ran nervous fingers through her hair, mussing it worse than he'd done, and straightened her clothes. She was breathing hard, her breasts rising and falling so dramatically that he was sure she was going to pop out of her teeny tank top.

Where had those plump breasts come from? He hadn't seen them earlier. Since he doubted Scarlet had given Lucy silicone implants, the breasts must have been there all along, hidden under the frumpy outfits.

"I really need to go to bed," she muttered, turning away. "I'm sure everything will make more sense in the morning. Oh, tomorrow remind me to bring you up to date on everything I told Scarlet. She was curious about me, and I'm afraid I just blathered the first thing that came into my mind."

"Like what?"

"Well, you and I met in Paris. I returned to my home in Kansas, burned all my clothes and traveled to New York, naked."

"What?"

"We'll talk about this tomorrow, okay? I really have to go to bed. G'night, Bryan, and thank you for everything." She grabbed her pile of clothes and fled, her sandals thunk-thunking against his wood floor as she headed for the guest room.

Traveled to New York, naked? What had possessed Lucy to say something like that? But since she'd said it, he couldn't get the picture out of his mind—Lucy boarding a plane, naked. Walking through the airport without a stitch on. Climbing into a cab—

No, he'd better not even go there. He was turned on enough already.

The woman was a siren, a witch. His groin ached with wanting her. Pretending to be besotted in front of others would be no problem—he was rapidly becoming obsessed. It was how to behave in private that would prove the problem.

He'd better just hold himself in check. Lucy was a key witness in what could ultimately prove to be a case of terrorism. He had no business kissing her or thinking about sleeping with her.

She'd said she was okay, that she could fake it. That had to be good enough. So, no more rehearsals. Professional, he had to be professional. He couldn't take advantage of a woman whose life had been turned upside down. She'd done the right thing for her country, and for her trouble she'd been spied on, lost her job and her home and couldn't contact anyone she knew. He was her anchor in a storm, and it would be easy for her to develop feelings all out of proportion.

He'd seen it happen before. He couldn't take advantage of her vulnerability. She didn't seem the casual-fling type, and that was all he could offer.

Lucy couldn't sleep, despite the fact she was exhausted. Her mind raced, reliving that kiss over and over, recalling every nuance of the pressure of his mouth on hers, the intoxicating warmth, the possessiveness, the feel of his hands in her hair and all over her.

She'd come alive like never before—not just her body or her hormones, but her whole being. The kiss had been…transcendental. She couldn't think of any other word to describe it.

Yet she knew that for him it was just another kiss. Rehearsal. Part of his business, his job. Keep the witness safe, make sure she knows her stuff, keep his family in the dark so they're safe, too.

She couldn't really blame him just because *she* reacted so profoundly to a simple kiss.

Her body still vibrated with the aftereffects, which only highlighted a sad fact about her life: for the past two years she'd been all but dead. A dull brain inside a dead shell, going through the motions, performing her job, staying out of trouble.

Only trouble had found her.

She might have been better off if none of this had happened. Maybe she'd have snapped out of her fugue on her own. Still, she couldn't say she was sorry to leave that life behind.

But she had to manage herself better. Not like when

she'd gone to work for the band. If she'd stuck to her guns back then, being satisfied simply to be on the fringes of that exciting world, she'd have been okay. Instead she'd deluded herself into thinking a million-aire rock star was going to marry her.

Her current situation wasn't so dissimilar. She'd again found herself on the fringes of an exciting world. This time it wasn't sex, drugs and rock 'n' roll, but spies, embezzlers and terrorists. Neither was a world she belonged in.

She had to remember that and not let herself get deluded into believing she was in any way special to Bryan, no matter what motions he went through.

Lucy eventually drifted off. When she awoke, daylight poured through her bedroom window, and a delicious smell tickled her nose. Whatever it was, it drew her out of bed like a black hole draws antimatter. She jumped in the shower, then stepped into a pair of white silk panties. Scarlet had given her about a dozen pair of the most delicious panties, all still in their packages. Apparently designers and clothing manufacturers sent freebies to the magazine all the time, hoping models or celebrities would wear them for photo shoots.

Lucy only had two of the magical push-up bras, though. When she'd seen the price tags on them, she'd nearly fainted. Who paid $80 for a bra? She would, she realized, now that she'd seen the miracle it performed.

Ordinarily, if she wasn't going to work, she'd put on a pair of jeans and a T-shirt. But Scarlet told her those clothes were out—they didn't go with "Lindsay's" new look. She would have to get used to wearing clingy knit pants and miniskirts, tiny crop-tops and blouses that revealed lots of skin.

She picked an outfit at random—a fawn-colored miniskirt and a fitted, sleeveless blouse with a subtle gold stripe. She didn't worry about makeup or jewelry—she would put them on only if she was appearing in public. She certainly didn't want Bryan to think she was trying too hard.

When she emerged from her bedroom and entered the kitchen, she found out what smelled so good. Bryan was making Belgian waffles, with fresh strawberries and real whipped cream.

"I'm going to be big as a house if you keep feeding me this way."

"Good morning to you, too." Bryan kept his attention on his cooking, never even glancing her way. "Sleep okay?"

No. I lay awake thinking about your blasted kiss. "Fine, thanks." She tried not to look at him, because if she did, she would think about kissing him. She couldn't help herself. He looked absolutely mouthwatering with his dark hair mussed, his face unshaven. He wore running shorts and a well-worn T-shirt with a Boca Royce Country Club logo on it. She recognized the name as an exclusive Manhattan club patronized by the very, very wealthy.

She was so in over her head.

He didn't look at her. He was busy filling mugs from a coffeemaker that looked like it belonged at NASA. The fragrance blended with the smell of waffles and strawberries, and her stomach growled.

"I've been out for a run—I do that most mornings," he said. "You can come with me. I also have a home gym."

Lucy had never been much of a jock before. "Maybe I should try running."

"If you like eating, it's a necessity."

She'd never been all that interested in food—maybe because she'd always had plenty. Growing up on a farm, the dinner table was loaded with meat, potatoes and fresh vegetables. But her mother had always urged her to eat more, claiming she was finicky as a cat.

When she'd hung out with In Tight, everyone had been more interested in drinking than eating, though there had always been something available—pizza or burgers. She'd eaten just enough to maintain her weight, so she hadn't ever felt the urge to work out.

Now she was ravenous. She dived into her waffle, savoring the pure maple syrup and the crunchy-outside, tender-inside texture. "Yeah, I'm going to have to do something, or all those pretty clothes Scarlet gave me won't look too hot."

"You can run with me tomorrow."

"I don't have any running shoes. Or gym clothes."

"You can buy some when we go out for your contact lenses."

She wondered how much money she had in her purse. Sixty dollars maybe, if she was lucky. "I can't use my credit cards, right?"

"No. No transactions involving your real name, for any reason. No telephone calls, either—not to anyone, even someone you think the bad guys would never be watching. I don't know the extent of their reach, but these guys are connected. Really connected."

That reminder brought Lucy back to earth in a hurry. She shivered as she thought about those "bad guys" in her apartment, searching through her things, listening to her on the phone.

When Bryan finished the last waffle, he popped it

onto a plate and finally spared a glance for Lucy. He did a double take.

"You can't expect me to be glamorous twenty-four hours a day," she groused. "Scarlet might have changed some of the trappings, but I'm still Lucy Miller."

"Did I complain?"

"No. But you were looking at me."

"I was looking because the clothes and hair color are still so different. I have to get used to them."

"Me, too. I hadn't realized how positively frumpy I'd become. But even in my wilder days, I still looked like me."

"You still look like you." He came and sat next to her at the bar, then leaned close enough that she could smell the faint scent brought on by his morning exertions. Not expensive cologne, but soap and sweat. A healthy, male scent. "Your smile is the same. You have a very pretty smile, only you don't use it enough."

"I don't have much to smile about." But that really wasn't true. Yes, she'd become the target of some unsavory people, and yes, she'd lost her job and her home and her very identity. But she just didn't care that much about those things. She was hanging out with a dangerously sexy spy and she was going to help him solve a crime. She had a wardrobe to die for and a personal-style consultant any woman in the world would give up her acrylic nails for.

"That's better," Bryan said, and Lucy realized she'd given him the requested smile.

Four hours later Lucy was in Victoria's Secret, feeling a bit like Julia Roberts in *Pretty Woman*. Bryan had taken her first to get the contacts. She'd been fitted on the spot with a pair of bright-green lenses, and she'd walked out of the optometrist's office feeling unburdened without the heavy glasses. She could see better, too. She'd forgotten how superior vision with contacts could be.

Next, Bryan had taken her shopping for all the things Scarlet hadn't provided—mostly athletic clothes. He'd bought her a pair of first-class Nike running shoes and a couple of color-coordinated designer outfits. She'd never worn designer clothing before yesterday, thinking it was silly to pay so much for a label. But she'd found out the clothes really were superior in quality. The fit and feel were fantastic.

She'd mentioned that she didn't have any sleepwear, so Bryan led her into the pricey lingerie store.

"We don't have to do anything this fancy," she protested. "You've already spent so much—"

"I can afford it. I want you comfortable, and you can't be comfortable in some cheap polyester pajamas."

"I can't be comfortable in a peek-a-boo nightie, either," she pointed out. But as she looked around, she realized the sleepwear here was gorgeous—not the least bit sleazy. She saw beautiful silk nightgowns in the most delicious pastels, but she also saw some pretty cotton nightshirts, and she knew that was what she should choose. Something supercomfortable.

"Uh-oh," Bryan muttered as she tried to find her size in a peach nightshirt.

Lucy's skin prickled with nerves. "What?" Had the bad guys tracked her down already? She glanced around, wondering if there was anyplace she could duck for cover if bullets started to fly.

"It's my stepmother. Of all people." He sounded disgusted. "Put down that nightshirt. I wouldn't buy a girlfriend anything like that. Here." He grabbed three skimpy nightgowns from a rack and thrust them at her. "Go try these on. Maybe you won't have to meet her. Oh, cripes, she's seen us. Too late."

The woman in question was petite and very thin, with unnaturally platinum hair in an expensive cut. She wore a pair of snug, low-rise jeans and a clingy shirt that looked pretty good on her surgically enhanced figure.

She might have been pretty but for the superior sneer on her face, which Lucy guessed was perpetual.

"Bryan, what on earth are you doing in a lingerie store?"

"Hi, Sharon," he said without much enthusiasm. The two didn't touch. "I'm buying a gift. This is Lindsay Morgan. Lindsay, my stepmother, Sharon Elliott."

Sharon nodded her acknowledgment while giving Lucy a thorough once-over. "Soon to be Sharon Styles again, thank God."

"It's nice to meet you," Lucy said politely. "Bryan, I'll just go try these on and give you two a chance to visit." And she scurried toward the dressing room, anxious to escape the obvious tension between Bryan and his stepmother. Her absence would also give Bryan a chance to explain her presence however he chose, without worrying she would say something to mess up his story. She was so new at this undercover thing, and she figured it was better if she got used to it in small doses. She hadn't forgotten the crazy story she'd blurted out to Scarlet, which they now had to live with.

When she got to the dressing room, she quickly undressed and tried on one of the silk nightgowns. Though Bryan had chosen the clothing at random, he'd gotten her size right, and the gown was absolutely gorgeous.

Without meaning to, she pictured herself wearing it in Bryan's loft. With Bryan looking on approvingly.

Though there was no one present to know her thoughts, her face flamed. She decided right then she would choose this gown—and a couple more just as sexy. She was done being frumpy, even if Bryan would never see the lovely scraps of silk on her.

"*Who* is *she?*" Sharon asked the moment she and Bryan were alone.

"I met her in Paris, but she's from Kansas," Bryan said, sticking to the story Lucy had told Scarlet. Although Sharon didn't have much contact with the family since the divorce proceedings had begun, she did talk to Bryan's father from time to time as they wrangled over the settlement details.

"And you're buying her lingerie?"

He shrugged. "Something wrong with a man buying his girlfriend lingerie?"

Sharon's eyebrows flew up. "Oh, so she's your girl-friend. I don't recall that you've had a girlfriend in a number of years." As if that made him suspect.

Bryan chose to let that comment pass. "Lindsay is pretty special."

"She seems very…sweet," Sharon said. "Well, I must get on with this. I've been invited to a wedding shower, and though I hate those things, it's at the Carlyle, and I heard there might be a couple of celebrities present."

That figured. Sharon had always been a social climber extraordinaire. She came from a wealthy fam-ily—Patrick had handpicked her for his son Daniel, after all. But her parents weren't famous-rich, like the Elliotts, and she'd reveled in her society-wife role, snubbing her old friends and collecting a new, richer batch. Now she was trying to elevate her status even higher.

He didn't dislike Sharon, for she'd been tolerant enough to him and his brother, Cullen, two boisterous stepsons. But she didn't give him any warm fuzzies, and she'd been pretty obstinate about the divorce.

She drifted away to shop, and Bryan found himself alone, staring at the wide array of sexy lingerie. Each thing he looked at—cach bra and panty set, each nightie, each thong—he couldn't help but picture on Lucy.

He'd been hoping last night was just a fluke, that he'd merely been turned on by the glamorous trappings Lucy had displayed. But when he'd seen her this morning, he'd known it was something far deeper than clothes or hair color that attracted him to Lucy Miller.

Lucy had an inner core of goodness that radiated from her. He'd never met anyone like her. He, on the other hand, was part of an ugly, shadowy world. Their two worlds were colliding, but that contact could only be temporary. She didn't belong in his, nor he in hers. He had to remember that.

Lucy reappeared a few minutes later. "Is she gone?"

He nodded. Sharon had grabbed a slinky black nightgown, paid for it and left without a backward glance. He wondered if she would find an excuse to call his dad and report what she'd seen. Despite the pending divorce, Sharon loved to gossip. "I'll put those up for you," he said to Lucy, holding out his arms. "You can go back to the nightshirts."

"No, thanks. I want these."

He looked again at the slinky, transparent fabrics

and daring, skin-revealing styles of the nightgowns she held, and his jeans grew noticeably tighter in the crotch. He did *not* need to think about Lucy wearing those!

Five

Lucy wore her ice-blue nightgown to bed that night. She felt sexy in it, which made her think of things she probably shouldn't. But she couldn't make herself clamp down on her fantasies. She'd spent two years seeing herself as a nonsexual being, and she didn't want to return to that. It was wonderful being able to *feel* again, even if some of those feelings were painful.

In the morning she dressed in a pair of pink exercise shorts, a sports bra, a pink tank top with the word Diva across the chest, and her new running shoes. She wore a terry sweatband to keep her hair out of her face.

Bryan was waiting for her when she emerged, grinding beans in his futuristic coffeepot.

"Ready?" he asked, looking pointedly at her bare legs. At least he wasn't focusing on her chest, or lack thereof. She'd gotten used to the cleavage her fancy push-up bras produced, but those bras weren't practical for running.

"I'm ready, but I warn you, I'm out of shape."

"We'll take it easy."

Five minutes later Lucy was thinking, If this is easy, I'd hate to see rigorous. She was huffing and puffing like a leaky accordion, her every muscle protesting. She'd had no idea she was in such bad condition.

To his credit, Bryan said nothing, just loped along beside her, breathing normally.

After a few minutes Lucy got into a rhythm and she felt a little better. She started to pay attention to the sights around her, the people hurrying to catch a bus or taxi, the bagel vendors, the honking horns and flocks of pigeons.

Oh, how she loved this city. She hadn't, however, often seen it at this hour of the morning. The In Tight crew was accustomed to starting the day around noon. Mornings, she discovered, had the same energy, but also a feeling of anticipation, of possibilities.

"You doing okay?" Bryan asked.

She nodded.

They veered into Central Park where they joined dozens of other morning joggers. Lucy dropped back a little so she could run behind Bryan and enjoy the view. He had the most gorgeous, tanned, muscular legs she'd ever seen, and a tight butt she wanted more than anything to grab. She giggled and almost choked to death because she didn't have the spare oxygen for laughter.

She stopped and coughed a few times, and Bryan, looking concerned, tapped her on the back until she was better.

"Maybe we should head back," he said.

She nodded, unable to speak.

"That was really good for a first time out."

She smiled at him, and he smiled back, and her heart did a little *plonk*. She wished he wouldn't be so nice to her. She wished she wasn't just a job to him, a responsibility to be taken care of. She wished they'd met some other way, and maybe they could go out on a date like normal people.

Her life was pretty far from normal.

She was sweating like an ox by the time they made it back to Bryan's building. Instead of going straight up, they swung into Une Nuit. Bryan introduced her to his manager, Stash, a charming man with a French accent who eyed her speculatively as Bryan put together a plate of pastries.

"This the one, eh?" he said.

"This is the one," Bryan confirmed, flashing a slightly embarrassed smile.

The one? What the heck did that mean?

Lucy looked around the huge commercial kitchen, which appeared to her like a forest of stainless steel, everything impeccably clean and sparkly. Three men and one woman wearing tall chef's hats bustled around preparing the day's menu, all joking and laughing in good-natured camaraderie.

This would be a fun place to work, she caught herself thinking. Not like Alliance Trust, where no one cracked a smile or spoke above a whisper, and the only smells were of new carpet and money. Honestly, that place was like a mausoleum.

"You want to see the rest of it?" Bryan asked, apparently noting her interest.

"Oh, yes, please."

He led her through a wide, swinging, double door into the main dining room, flipping on a couple of light switches as they went. The decor was nothing short of seductive. Low red lighting illuminated the copper-topped tables, which were surrounded by black suede banquettes and armchairs. Tables and booths were tucked away at odd angles in little corners, and she imagined the famous people who ate here enjoyed the sense of privacy.

The floor was black-and-red stone—marble, or maybe something else. Contemporary wrought-iron chandeliers hung here and there, each one different, each one a work of art.

"Wow, this is beautiful. Did you decorate it yourself?"

"No, I hired a design firm. They did my loft, too. I can't take credit for that. Except some of the artwork."

"It's wonderful. Can we eat here some time?" She nearly swooned at the idea of an intimate dinner with Bryan. Since they would be in public, they would have to act like a couple in love. It wouldn't be too difficult for her.

"You can eat here anytime you like. Stash will take care of you."

That wasn't really what she wanted to hear. She wanted Bryan to be the one taking care of her. They could share a plate of crepes stuffed with stir-fry—or whatever exotic thing was on the menu—and feed each other with chopsticks.

Bryan showed her the bar area, which featured smaller tables and less-cushy chairs, for those waiting for a table or just stopping in for a cocktail.

"Downstairs there's a private dining room, for parties and such. Do you want to see it?"

She glanced at her watch. "I suppose we better get going. I have a lot of work to do on the computer today."

They went upstairs, showered, then met again in the kitchen to gobble down the French pastries and coffee. Yes, she was going to have to make running a habit.

Hours later Lucy was firmly ensconced in Bryan's private study, which was upstairs off the master suite. The door had been locked the night Scarlet came over— Lucy had checked the door out of curiosity. But this morning he'd let her in, fired up his computer and put her to work. She had not only the memory stick she'd taken with her when she fled from D.C., but all of the data she'd provided Brian with over the past few weeks. He had been going over it himself, along with some of Homeland Security's top computer experts, but none of them had been able to figure out who was siphoning money out of the pension funds. The embezzling had been disguised to look like ordinary transactions. Fund managers bought and sold stock and securities all the time. Only by comparing the transactions with the various fund managers' portfolio profiles could the bogus stock sales be ferreted out.

For the past three hours, Lucy had been going over personal e-mails. She felt terrible for invading her co-workers' privacy, but Bryan had assured her it was both legal and necessary. The embezzler wasn't operating in a vacuum. Maybe he wasn't stupid enough to leave in-criminating evidence in an e-mail—but maybe he was.

Bryan had left her alone to attend to his own business. He was checking in with the other agents on his team to see if any progress had been made from their ends. When she heard footsteps coming up the stairs,

Lucy was almost giddy at the prospect of seeing him again. She told herself it was only because she was anxious to report what she'd found. But deep down she knew it was more than that. She was forming an unhealthy attachment to her superspy, which was only going to lead to pain and disappointment.

But what could she do? She couldn't order her emotions to behave. And her hormones were completely out of her control.

Bryan entered the study, and Lucy's smile died. The strain on his face was obvious. "Bad news?"

"One of the agents on my team is MIA."

"Oh, no, that's awful!"

"No one has heard from him in three days."

"What do you think happened? Where was he the last time you knew?"

"He's been in France. He infiltrated the bogus charity your embezzler has been funneling money to, and was tracing down wire transfers that matched the amounts we know were stolen from Alliance at certain times. But now he's vanished. Either he's blown his cover…or he's the traitor. But I find that impossible to believe. I've worked closely with Stungun on two other missions. I'd have trusted him with my life anyday."

"Stungun?"

Bryan rolled his eyes. "We all have code names. We don't know each other's real names. Not even my superior knows who I am."

"What are the other agents' code names?"

"My team consists of me, Stungun, Tarantula and Orchid. Siberia is our control—our boss."

"It's okay for you to tell me that?"

He smiled briefly. "We change the code names all the

time. I'm Casanova right now, but I've been Jackknife, Hustler and Hopper."

"Hopper?"

He shrugged. "'Cause I'm quick like a rabbit, I guess. I didn't come up with it." He sat wearily in a leather office chair. "Have you found anything?"

"You wouldn't believe what I've found out. John Pelton, one of our loan officers, has been downloading porn. Really raunchy stuff. I *never* would have guessed. Then there's Cassie Hall and Peter Glass. They've apparently been carrying on a torrid affair—and they're both married to other people! I feel like a pervert, reading their e-mails."

"Anything pertinent to the case?"

"I've been comparing log-ins to the times various illegal transactions were made. It's painstakingly slow, but I think I might be able to figure out who the culprit is by process of elimination."

"Any front runners?"

"I've been able to eliminate a couple of people. But there are still dozens of candidates. Most people stay logged in all day when they're at work. Still, it's a start."

"Good. Keep at it. There are cold cuts and fruit in the fridge if you're hungry."

She glanced at her watch and was surprised to see it was almost two. She'd been so engrossed in solving the puzzle, she'd been oblivious to the passage of time.

"I'm afraid I have more bad news," he said, his tone positively funereal.

"What? It's not my family, is it? They haven't reported me missing or anything, I hope." She wasn't in close contact with her parents—she talked to them every couple of weeks. They wouldn't be worried about her yet.

When he didn't answer at once, she felt panic creeping over her. "Bryan? What is it?"

"It's my grandparents. They're holding a dinner tonight at their house on Long Island. It's a command performance. We have to be there."

"Oh." Word had apparently gotten out about Bryan's new girlfriend, and she was being summoned for inspection.

"The good news is," he continued, "my cousins and aunts and uncles will be there, and they're all at each other's throats these days, so there'll be lots of drama to keep everyone distracted. The focus won't be solely on you—though you'll receive your share. Are you up to it?"

"Sure. As long as no one asks me how I got from Kansas to New York with no clothes."

Bryan waited nervously in the living room while Lucy got ready for dinner at The Tides, the home where he'd spent a lot of his growing-up years. She'd been very nervous about what to wear when he'd told her the Elliotts dressed for dinner.

His grandparents could be a bit pretentious, no two ways about it. And controlling? They gave new meaning to the word. The competition Patrick Elliott had set up among his children and grandchildren was a perfect example. He liked to make them jump through hoops.

Still, they were good people, and they wanted what they thought was best for their loved ones.

When Bryan heard Lucy's bedroom door open and shut, his gaze went immediately to the corner around which he knew she would soon appear, and he caught himself holding his breath. Having seen some of the clothing Scarlet had picked out for his "girlfriend," he couldn't wait to see how Lucy had tricked herself out tonight.

He wasn't disappointed. When she came around the corner, she wore a clingy halter dress in a muted, burnt-orange color. It came almost to her knees, the hem ending in a flirty little ruffle, but that didn't make it conservative. It showed every delicious curve of her body. She'd draped a silk fringed shawl over her bare shoulders, the color ranging from pale peach to a dark orange. A bold silver necklace called attention to her long neck and the enticing curve of her breasts.

"Too slutty?" she asked. "I don't want your family to think I'm easy, although if I've moved in with you after knowing you only a couple of weeks, I guess I must be."

"You look terrific, not slutty at all." He wanted to touch her. He wanted to untie the little bow at the back of her neck and peel that dress right down to her waist. He wanted to kiss the shiny gloss off her lips and tease her breasts until her nipples were hard against his palms—

"Bryan?"

"What?"

"Shouldn't we go? I don't want to be late."

Bryan forced himself to think about the time he'd crash-landed a plane in a Greenland blizzard and had survived for two days on four granola bars. Cold, very, very cold. He'd gotten frostbite and had almost lost his little toe.

Better. "Yes, let's go." He offered her his arm in a courtly gesture, and she took it, smiling uncertainly. "You look like a goddess, you know."

"Oh, stop."

"You do. And it's not just the designer clothes and trendy hair. Since your makeover, you carry yourself differently."

"It's my inner Lindsay," she quipped, though he could tell she was pleased with the compliment.

On the drive out to Long Island, Lucy worked at memorizing their story. They'd met at a Paris café where Bryan was swapping recipes with a chef. She'd gone there thinking she would write a novel but had found out she couldn't write. Now she was trying to find herself. She'd inherited a bit of money and so was in no hurry to get a job.

They invented fake names for her parents and a fake Kansas town as her home.

"You can say you worked at a bank, since you know that world, but make it somewhere besides D.C."

"What about my education? I have a finance degree."

"Keep it, but say you went to…I don't know. Loyola. None of my family has ever been near Chicago."

"I'll just try to steer conversation away from me. I'll ask questions about you instead. That worked pretty well with Scarlet."

"Oh, really? And what did Scarlet say about me?"

Lucy put on her most innocent face. "She said when you were a kid you liked to pull the wings off flies and burn things."

"What?" The look on his face was priceless.

"I'm kidding. She said you were the only one who didn't go into the magazine business. Why is that?"

"I'd planned to. I actually studied finance, with some vague idea of working in the EPH home office. But the government recruited me before I graduated. I knew I couldn't tell my family I was training to be a spy— they'd have gone through the roof. So I bought a restaurant instead."

"Why a restaurant?"

"I met Stash when I was still in school. It was his dream, and I knew I liked food. So I bought the café and hired him to run it. I had no idea I would enjoy it so much. I'd planned on being more of a silent owner, but it hasn't worked out that way."

"Tell me more about your family. Who will be there tonight, besides your grandparents?"

"No telling. Most of the family comes when Granddad calls, unless they're testifying before the Supreme Court or vacationing in Sri Lanka. But with everyone so tense these days, I'm not sure."

"Will either of your parents be there?"

"Not Mom. She doesn't set foot at The Tides. Dad will probably be there, though."

"Your parents don't get along, then?" Lucy was saddened at the thought of Bryan and his brother growing up with two feuding parents. Scarlet had let it slip that Bryan's parents had split when he was about twelve.

"Oh, no, actually they get along fine. It's Patrick my mom can't stand."

"Your grandfather?"

He nodded. "I don't think she's spoken to him since I was a kid. She's kept in touch with my aunt Karen, but no one else in the family."

"Why the feud?" Lucy wanted to know.

Bryan shrugged. "She never said, but I think she blames Granddad for the divorce somehow. Like I said, he is controlling. And when I was— Well, you don't want to hear all that."

"I do, really. Unless you'd rather not."

He continued only reluctantly. "When I was a kid, I had to have an operation—the kind our insurance wouldn't pay for because it was considered experimental. Granddad paid for it—and I'll be forever grateful to him, because it saved my life, literally. But I think he felt my parents owed him after that, and he used that debt to keep them under his thumb. Ultimately, I think that's what caused the divorce."

Bryan looked so sad, almost shattered, that Lucy reached over and laid her hand on his arm. "Surely you don't blame yourself. You were just a little boy. You had no control over a health problem."

"I know. But the fact remains, if I hadn't gotten sick, our lives would have been a lot different."

"And maybe you wouldn't have pushed yourself to become a super athlete, and you wouldn't have been recruited by the CIA, and you wouldn't have been assigned to my case, and whoever was watching me would have killed me. You can't play the what-if game. It's silly."

He looked over at her and smiled. "You're an amazing woman, Lucy Miller." He took her hand and squeezed it, then didn't let it go.

"Lindsay Morgan." She felt the warmth of his touch all the way to her heart. If it felt this fantastic when he touched her hand, what would it be like if he touched her other places?

Don't go there.

He only released her hand when he had to shift gears, downshifting as he reached their destination.

The Elliott home was in the Hamptons, where else? Lucy had been to the Hamptons a few times for some wild parties, so she thought she knew what to expect. But The Tides, as it was called, shocked her nonetheless. The turn-of-the-century mansion—no other word for it—was perched on a cliff above the shore. To get to it, Bryan turned his Jaguar down a private drive, where a guard waved him through.

"A gated community," Lucy said. "Nice."

"Not a community. Just one house."

"You mean that security guard sits there all the time to guard just one house?"

"That's right."

Lucy thought she'd seen wealth and opulence, but she was afraid her preconceived notions hadn't prepared her for the Elliott estate. As the perfectly manicured grounds passed by outside the car window, she wondered how she would measure up. Designer clothes and a chic haircut didn't change the fact she was a farm girl from Kansas.

The house up close was even more impressive than from a distance. The rusty sandstone monolith came into view as they rounded the last corner and drove onto the circular drive, and it literally took Lucy's breath away. The high, peaked roof was gray slate, and there were so many gables and turrets and cupolas and multipaned windows that Lucy's head spun.

"Wow."

Bryan laughed. "I loved this place growing up. Always so full of activity, laughing, fighting. Granddad has talked about downsizing now that it's just the two of them most of the time, but I doubt they'll ever do it. Gram loves this place too much. She says the grounds remind her of Ireland."

Other cars had already arrived. Bryan parked and came around to open Lucy's door, but she was already out of the car by the time he arrived. Again he offered her his arm. "Remember, we're smitten."

As if she had to struggle too hard. They walked up the brick stairs to the porch. Not standing on ceremony, Bryan opened the door and ushered her inside a marble foyer with a crystal chandelier twenty people could have swung from. Straight ahead was a formal living room; to the right, Lucy glimpsed a dining room with a massive table already set with linens, china, crystal.

Despite the luxury, the house exuded a welcoming warmth. Elegant and understated, the decor didn't scream professional decorator. Instead Lucy was willing to bet the lady of the house had decorated it herself. There were family photos and knickknacks everywhere, arranged in attractive groupings. The furniture, while upholstered in stylish colors, appeared to have been chosen for comfort and sturdiness.

A group was already seated in the living room, and the murmured conversation stopped the moment Bryan and Lucy entered. They all looked expectantly at the newcomers.

"Bryan." A handsome man in his forties bounded up and approached Bryan with a hearty handshake. He looked too young to be Bryan's father, but with the physical likeness between the two men, they couldn't be anything but father and son.

He focused on Lucy. "And you must be Lindsay. I'm Daniel Elliott, Bryan's father."

They shook hands. "I guessed as much."

"Everyone," Bryan said, "this is Lindsay Morgan. I would appreciate it if you didn't scare her to death.

Remember, the Elliotts en masse can be a trifle intim-idating."

Lucy was introduced to each Elliott in turn. His brother, Cullen, was easy to remember, because he looked enough like Bryan to be a twin. Cullen's wife, Misty, was also memorable, mostly because she was close to six feet tall, pregnant and amazingly gorgeous.

Scarlet she knew, of course, but now she met her fiancé, John Harlan, an ad exec. And Scarlet's twin sister, Summer, who was a carbon copy, if a tad less flamboyant. Summer's fiancé, Zeke Woodlow, made a definite impression. Who could forget him? He was a rock star, and a golden god of a man even when he wasn't assuming his stage persona. He and Summer were on a break from touring, Summer explained, while she and her twin planned their double wedding.

But after a while, the names and faces began to blur. Trying to remember her cover story *and* commit names to memory proved too much for Lucy's little brain. It wouldn't matter in the long run, she told herself. In a matter of weeks she would be gone, hardly a blip on the collective memory of the Elliott clan.

But it did matter. She wanted the Elliotts to like her. She wanted to be a positive reflection on Bryan.

Finally Bryan's grandparents appeared. Lucy had never met a more intimidating man than Patrick Elliott. Though well into his seventies, he was still strong and vital, and it was clear his word was law around here.

"So you're the new girlfriend," he said, giving her a once-over as if she were a horse he'd bought at auction.

Bryan made polite introductions, but Patrick didn't do anything so modern as shake Lucy's hand. He nodded brusquely.

"Don't mind him," said Maeve, Bryan's grandmother. She was a petite woman and still a beauty. Her mostly white hair, piled up on her head in an elegant upsweep, carried traces of auburn, and her nose bore a sprinkling of pale freckles. Her green eyes were sharp as a bird's and missed nothing. "He's a gruff old goat, but deep down he's a charmer. Welcome to The Tides, Lindsay."

Maeve grasped both Lucy's hands and squeezed them, and Lucy instantly fell in love with the woman. She was just adorable.

Though Lucy quickly ceased to be the center of attention, she could sense the Elliotts watching her at various times. When others arrived—Bryan's uncle Shane and his cousin Teagan and Teagan's fiancée, Renee—conversations broke into small groups, and the talk focused on the magazines. Which was only natural, since almost all of them worked for EPH.

Even an outsider could see the tensions. Those who worked for the same magazine flocked together, sometimes with heads bent low. Sometimes voices were raised, then boisterous laughter would break out, a spontaneous hug here and there.

Lucy wasn't used to any family showing their feelings so freely. In the home where she'd grown up, she'd been taught to keep emotions in check. Voices were never raised, laughter seldom heard. And hugging? Forget it.

No wonder Lucy had rebelled so far in the other direction, allowing her life to get about as messy as one could get.

"Let me refill that wine, Lindsay," Daniel said. "Which one were you drinking?"

"Uh, red?"

"Burgundy? Or was it the pinot noir?"

Lucy felt sure she should know the difference, but she didn't. Her parents hadn't allowed alcohol in their house, and In Tight had leaned toward beer and the hard stuff.

At her clueless expression, Daniel took her elbow and led her to the bar, where several bottles were lined up. "This is the burgundy," he said, "a particularly nice one from Australia. The pinot noir is a Chilean variety. Dry, but with a hint of floral and oak." He smiled at her. "Pretend you're interested in my boring dissertation on wine, okay? Make me look good."

Lucy laughed. "I am interested. I just don't know much about wine. I think I drank from the bottle with the green label."

He picked up the bottle and refilled her glass. "Actually, I have an ulterior motive in cutting you out from the herd. I wanted to have a private word with you."

Uh-oh, here it comes, Lucy thought, tamping down her panic. Bryan's father had picked up on something out of kilter. She'd blown it.

"I'm very worried about Bryan. He's been traveling so much lately. And when he showed up for his brother's wedding here in May, he had a split lip and a limp. He claimed he was in a car accident, but his car didn't have a scratch on it."

This was all news to Lucy. She looked up at him blankly.

"You mean, you don't know?"

"We haven't been dating for long," she said, her voice shaking with nerves. "It's been a real whirlwind. I still have so much to learn about Bryan. He hasn't mentioned any car accident." All of which was true.

"I feel like he's hiding something. And I'm not just being a paranoid dad. His mother is worried, too. And Cullen. We all feel like he's not being honest with us. Maybe trying to protect us."

Oh, dear. How was she supposed to respond to that?

She wanted to tell Daniel not to worry, but in good conscience, she couldn't. Bryan was in danger almost all the time. She wanted to reassure Daniel that Bryan wasn't involved in something nefarious, that he wasn't embroiled in trouble. She couldn't do that, either.

"Bryan is a very private person," she finally said.

"But what was he doing in France? Surely it couldn't take weeks and weeks to swap recipes."

Bryan had told her to stick to the truth as much as possible. But she knew nothing about what he did in France. She shrugged helplessly. "He was meeting with all kinds of people."

"You mean like chefs and restaurant managers and spice dealers?"

And terrorists and spies. She nodded.

"Well, maybe there's more to running a restaurant than I thought. Maybe now that he has a girlfriend, he'll stay home more. You'll take good care of him, won't you?"

"More like he's taking good care of me."

Six

Dinner was the typical five-course extravaganza. Though the Elliotts had a chef come in even for their family dinners, Maeve was a fine cook in her own right and couldn't resist dabbling in the kitchen. The meal tonight was vichyssoise, followed by a field-green salad, braised salmon, beef tips with fresh asparagus, and fudge-caramel mousse.

"What do you think, Bryan, love?" Maeve asked. "Up to your standards?"

"Gram, you know even Une Nuit can't compete with the dinners you serve here," he said diplomatically. He'd enjoyed the dinner but he'd spent most of his time watching Lucy, who was so nervous she could hardly swallow. She was doing a spectacular job posing as Lindsay. She'd often shot him nervous but affectionate looks throughout the evening, and a couple of times she'd sought him out and taken his hand.

He had to admit, the feel of her smooth little hand in his had stirred something inside him until it was becoming increasingly difficult to separate fact from fiction. But that was the general idea when working a cover story. Live it, believe it, and you could be convincing.

But was he living it a little too much? He certainly had no problem doting on "Lindsay." He even stole the cherry from the top of the mousse and presented it to her, which started a boisterous argument among the cousins. When they'd been kids, they'd always fought over the cherry until Maeve had been forced to go to the kitchen and bring out the jar of maraschinos, giving each of her grandkids one.

"So," Patrick said, "where is your twin sister this evening, Shane?"

"Why are you asking me?" said Shane, who was editor in chief of *The Buzz*. "You know Fin. She's eating and sleeping at *Charisma* these days, she's so obsessed with this competition."

The others at the table agreed. This was one of those times Bryan was truly grateful not to be in the magazine business. He didn't like this competition among his aunt, uncles and cousins for control of EPH. He had no idea what his grandfather's goal had been in setting up the contest, but surely it wasn't to put them all at each other's throats.

"No need to criticize," said Scarlet, sticking up for her boss. "Aunt Finny is devoted, that's all. She truly cares about *Charisma*."

"Oh, and I don't care about *The Buzz?*" Shane shot back.

"I didn't say that."

More arguments broke out after that. Bryan leaned back and folded his arms, rather enjoying the melee. The things some people thought were important.

Lucy interrupted his amusement. "Excuse me," she said quietly to him. "I'll be back."

He thought she'd just gone to the powder room, but when she hadn't returned in ten minutes, he started to worry. Maeve had brought out the dessert, and Lucy's sat untouched.

Realistically, Bryan knew nothing could happen to Lucy while she was at The Tides. The place was safe as Fort Knox. But her absence made him uneasy, and he excused himself to go look for her.

The downstairs guest bath door was open, the light off. If she'd ever been there, she wasn't there now.

He wandered all around the first floor, thinking maybe she'd gotten distracted by his grandparents' artwork or knickknacks, some of which were museum quality. But she was nowhere.

Surely she hadn't gone upstairs. Unless she'd felt ill and wanted to lie down. But wouldn't she have said something to him?

He checked upstairs and still didn't find her. Now he was truly worried.

He returned to the dining room. Her chair remained empty.

"Bryan?" his grandmother inquired. "Something wrong?"

"I seem to have lost my girlfriend."

"We probably upset her with all our arguing," Scarlet said. "Bryan was right when he said we could be scary."

Scary, maybe, but his family stuck together in a crisis. And though this didn't exactly qualify as a crisis yet, the others didn't hesitate to put down their dessert spoons, push back from the table and go in search of Bryan's lost date.

He found her a couple of minutes later. Theorizing that she might have stepped outside for a breath of fresh air, he went out to the patio, then to the steps that had been carved out of the cliff leading down to the private beach. He spotted a solitary figure, standing on the sand below looking out to sea, and his whole body relaxed with relief.

He stepped back inside to let the others know he'd found her. Then he went down to the beach.

She didn't hear him over the waves until he was almost upon her. She turned, startled, and her cheeks were wet with tears.

"Lucy, what on earth is wrong?"

She swiped at one cheek with the back of her hand and laughed self-consciously. "I'm sorry. I didn't mean to worry you. I only intended to step outside for a minute. My head was spinning. I shouldn't have had that third glass of wine."

"It's us who should be apologizing, arguing like that when we have guests. I'm sorry if we upset you."

She laid a hand on his arm. "I didn't mind the arguing. That's not it."

"Then what is it?" he asked, bewildered. But then again, most women bewildered him. They were such complex creatures.

"I was just thinking how fun it would be to belong to a big, boisterous family like the Elliotts. And that got me to thinking about my family. We don't fight, true, but that's because we hardly ever talk. And of all stupid things, I sort of started to miss my parents. And I started thinking, if I don't make it through this—"

"Make it through?" He couldn't help it, he had to interrupt. "Lucy, you'll make it through. It may take time, but look at the progress we've made already."

"I told you I was being silly."

"I know this thing has turned your life upside down. I admire the fact you were brave enough to take on embezzlers and terrorists. Not everyone would do that."

She shrugged.

"I'll get you back home to your normal life as soon as possible," he said, though he didn't look forward to pushing her out of his life. But that was inevitable. Tempted though he was, he couldn't allow Lucy or any woman to get close to him. It wasn't fair and it wasn't safe.

"It certainly hasn't been all bad," she said with a sniff. The ocean breeze had all but dried her tears. "At home I don't get to dress like this or have dinner at a gazillion-dollar mansion or meet publishing luminaries."

"Publishing luminaries with bad manners," Bryan added with a rueful laugh. "Ah, Lucy, you're a good sport."

He gave her a spontaneous hug, which he'd intended to be brief and brotherly. Instead, Lucy put her arms around him and hugged him back, hard, pressing her luscious body against his.

Almost of its own accord, his hand slid down to her slender waist, then lower, flirting with the curve of her bottom.

When he realized what he was doing he froze. He'd been about to grab Lucy's butt! He forced himself to ease his grip on her, to gradually pull away.

She looked up at him with those vibrant green eyes

still dewy with tears, her pink mouth slightly parted. And the expression in her eyes, one of such utter trust, did him in completely.

No one had ever looked at him that way. Before he knew what was happening, he bent his head and closed the few inches between them, capturing those moist, pink lips with his.

Her lips were rose-petal soft, and as open and giving as a rose in full bloom, too. Bryan's energy collided and melded with Lucy's as their vibrations became one, breathing and heartbeats in sync, until he wasn't sure where he ended and she began.

His body, which had been tuned to Lucy's station almost from the moment they met, leaped to life with a craving so keen it was painful.

She tasted faintly of the wine she'd been drinking, and he tasted more deeply, coaxing her with his tongue to open even more. She did without hesitation. Again the utter trust she showed blew him away.

It was that trust that finally dragged him to his senses. He could not take advantage of this situation. He'd gotten Lucy into her current position and had promised to protect her. She was depending on him for everything—food, clothing, shelter. To abuse his position was unconscionable.

He pulled back again, and this time he put his hands on her bare arms and gently pushed her away as he broke the kiss.

"We shouldn't do this."

She blinked a couple of times, and he wondered if he imagined the hurt look in her eyes. But in the span of another heartbeat, she smiled mischievously. "Why not? We're supposed to be smitten. I was just playing the part."

"Honey, if that was acting, you deserve an Academy Award."

"I'm very talented," she agreed, leaving him to wonder what exactly she meant by that. A talented actress? Or talented in other ways?

As they turned toward the staircase, Lucy boldly put her hand on his butt and squeezed. "Very talented."

So, no ambiguity there. She'd practically issued an engraved invitation that she was open to making love.

Regrettably, it was one invitation he was going to have to decline. But that didn't mean he couldn't think about it—which he did, through the remainder of dessert and after-dinner coffee, through the farewell hugs and promises to drive carefully, and throughout the drive home.

He was as primed as a sixteen-year-old on his first car date—and unfortunately about as likely to get lucky. Every time he glanced over at her, her blond hair swirling about her face from the breeze coming through the moon roof, her eyes drowsy from good food and wine and pure exhaustion, he wanted to come out of his skin.

He escorted her to the elevator in his building, careful not to touch her. "I'll be up in a few minutes," he said. "I need to check on things at the restaurant."

She glanced at her watch. "Isn't the restaurant closed?"

"Uh, right. I need to be sure things are ready for to-morrow." Which was a silly reply, because Lucy knew Stash took care of the day-to-day concerns. But it was the best he could come up with. He couldn't possibly go up to his apartment with her until he had his libido under control. In his current state, she had only to hint at seduction and he would be at her mercy. Seeing as how he didn't know what she had in mind, he thought it would be safer to keep his distance.

"All right. Well, I guess I'll see you tomorrow, then."

"Tomorrow. Oh, and Lucy, you did great tonight. Posing as Lindsay, I mean. I don't think anyone in my family suspects a thing."

"I'm not so sure about that, but thanks."

He gave the verbal command that would send the elevator up to his loft, then stepped out and let the doors close between them.

He used his key to get into the darkened restaurant. What he needed was to burn off excess energy, and whipping something up in the kitchen ought to do the trick, he thought. Something decadent, something with chocolate and bourbon, the best substitutes for sex he could think of.

Maeve had given him his love for fine food. When his brother and cousins were outside playing and he couldn't join in because of his heart ailment, Maeve would take him into the kitchen. He would pick out a recipe from her many boxes and cookbooks, and together they would cook. He learned to associate the heady smells of yeast and chocolate and toasted almonds with happy times, and to this day puttering in the kitchen could take the edge off when he was tense, or when he had to figure something out.

His plan was to dream up a new dessert and play around with the ingredients while he put some serious thought to how to track down Stungun—and either rescue him, find out who killed him—or bring him to justice if he was the traitor.

Instead, his thoughts turned again and again to Lucy—how she'd looked on the beach with the wind in her hair and her clothes molded against her body, the strength in her stance and the vulnerability in her face, her intelligence and bravery.

Soon he had three different sauces on the stove and he was going to work on some heavy cream with the KitchenAid mixer. An orange cake was in the oven—not one of these fluffy, melt-in-your-mouth cakes, but something with some substance. He didn't yet know what the end product would be, but he planned to eat the whole thing himself, until his appetites were subdued—or he was too sick to even think about making love to Lucy. Only then could he return to his apartment.

Lucy lay in her bed in one of her slinky new nighties, trying her best to find sleep. But she couldn't help thinking about the kiss on the beach.

That kiss had been no acting job, on her part or Bryan's. She'd tasted the naked desire in the kiss, sharp as a knife and strong as a tidal wave. She'd felt the answering call in herself, a yearning so strong she couldn't deny it. She'd floated on air the rest of the long evening at The Tides, unbothered now by the Elliotts' noisy bickering, not nervous about carrying off her role as Lindsay Morgan. She'd played her part well—really well, apparently, given what was happening between herself and Bryan.

The only question left was, would they act on the waves of desire coursing between them?

She knew she wanted to, and she'd let Bryan know her feelings in no uncertain terms. But she still wasn't sure what he wanted. He hadn't said a word about it during the silent drive home.

Now, as the minutes clicked by on her bedside clock,

it became more and more evident that he wouldn't come to her. He was staying away on purpose, trying to avoid any awkward good-night scenes.

She knew that for him to make love to her would cross an ethical boundary, and she respected Bryan's wish not to mix his professional life with his personal.

But how often did two people resonate the way she and Bryan did? How did one simply turn one's back on those feelings?

She couldn't do it.

When more than an hour had passed, Lucy's frustrations turned to worry. What was keeping him? What could he possibly have to check on at the restaurant that would take this long? Had something happened to him?

When she couldn't stand not knowing any longer, Lucy got out of bed and threw on a pair of warmup pants and a T-shirt. Hardly clothing designed for seduction, but seduction was far from her mind now. She put on her glasses—a new, more stylish pair with lightweight lenses Bryan had insisted on when they'd ordered her contacts—and headed for the elevator.

She could get out of Bryan's apartment, but unless she found him, she couldn't get back in. So she took a few dollars with her and Scarlet's phone number, in case she got locked out. Then she got in the elevator and headed down to the restaurant level.

The restaurant had been dark when they'd arrived home, but she could see a light coming from somewhere now. She tried the door. It was locked, so she banged loudly.

At first no one came, and Lucy envisioned the worst—Bryan lying on the floor in a pool of blood, helpless to answer her knock. But finally she saw a shadowy figure approaching. Apprehension seized her, followed quickly by a rush of relief when the figure resolved into Bryan's familiar form.

He turned the dead bolt and opened the door. "Lucy, what are you doing here?"

"I couldn't sleep. I was worried about you when you didn't come back." She realized how stupid that sounded. She was worried about a superspy, so she was coming downstairs to rescue him?

He smiled indulgently at her. "Thank you for worrying. And I'm sorry, but I got caught up—"

"What is that smell?" she demanded, cutting him off. She yanked the door open wide enough that she could slide inside past Bryan. The smell coming from the kitchen drew her like the pied piper's music.

"It's just a…dessert."

"After all the food we ate at your grandparents' house, you were hungry?" But even as she said that, her own stomach growled, reacting to the commingled scents. Whatever was cooking, she wanted some of it.

"Cooking helps me think," he said.

She zeroed in on the tall cake sitting on a cooling rack. "Orange, that's what I smell."

"Right. It's an orange pound cake."

"And chocolate. And…bourbon?"

"You have a good nose."

"What is this dessert?" she asked, intrigued.

"I don't know yet. I'm making it up as I go along."

Lucy inspected the sauces slowly simmering on the stove, taking a good whiff of each one. Her mouth watered. Unable to resist, she dipped a finger in the warm chocolate sauce and took a taste.

"Mmmm."

"Lucy! This is a restaurant. You can't do that."

"You're not actually going to serve that cake to patrons, are you?"

"I can't now." But he grinned. "Actually, I was planning to eat the whole thing myself."

"Not without my help, you don't. What comes next?"

She watched as Bryan used a very sharp knife to cut the cake into four layers, all perfectly uniform. "You're good with a knife," she said.

"I'm good with all my tools," he replied, paying her back for her saucy comments on the beach earlier.

"I'll bet you are."

He gave her a warning look, then returned his attention to the cake. He spread fresh whipped cream on the bottom layer, then spooned on some of the chocolate sauce and set the second layer on top. Then came more whipped cream and the bourbon sauce, and another layer. Yet more whipped cream, more chocolate sauce, and some toasted almonds, and the final layer.

"I want to drizzle a glaze on top, but I'm not sure what to flavor it with. Lemon?"

Lucy shook her head. "Too much citrus. I don't know what I'm talking about, but how about crème de menthe? When I was little, I used to mix orange sherbet with mint-chocolate-chip ice cream."

"You innovator, you." He grinned. "Okay, what the hell." He quickly mixed up a glaze, adding a dash of spearmint extract rather than crème de menthe, which he thought might compete with the bourbon. He garnished the cake with orange slices and sprigs of fresh mint.

"It's the most beautiful cake I've ever seen," she said reverently.

"You're not laying it on a little thick, are you?"

"No. It's a work of art. Shame to cut into it. But you are going to cut into it, aren't you?" she asked anxiously.

In answer he got out two plates, then wielded his knife and spatula to cut two perfectly uniform slices, which he laid on the plates sideways. He topped each with another small dollop of whipped cream and a mint leaf.

"Presentation is everything."

Lucy knew she should be admiring the dessert. But she'd eyed a small spot of whipped cream on Bryan's cheek, and she became fixated on it.

"What?" he asked.

"You have whipped cream on your face."

"Oh." He rubbed one side of his face with the dishcloth he kept over one shoulder, missing the spot completely.

"Here, let me." She took the dishcloth from him. But instead of wiping his face, she stood on her tiptoes and licked off the whipped cream.

Bryan's pupil dilated. "Oh, Lucy." His voice was hoarse with suppressed passion. They were standing near the stove, and Lucy reached over to the pan of chocolate sauce, dipped her finger in again, and wiped a little on his other cheek before sucking the end of her finger.

"You do get dirty when you cook, don't you?" She again stretched up on tiptoe so she could dart her tongue out and lick off the chocolate.

"You are a very wicked girl." He dipped a finger into the bowl of whipped cream and spread a smear across her lips. "Oh, dear, look, I've made another mess."

Lucy reflexively licked at the whipped cream, but Bryan shook his head. "No, no, you've missed most of it." He leaned down and claimed her lips with his.

The kiss started out light and teasing, but it didn't

stay that way. His mouth went hard, demanding, his breathing harsh and rapid, and Lucy drank it in, his passion elevating hers.

She hadn't meant to come in here and seduce him. Not exactly, anyway, but clearly that was what she'd done. And this time they were not in a public place, there was no family nearby. They were in a deserted restaurant with just the heady scents of chocolate and orange surrounding them.

Bryan's kisses moved from her mouth to her jaw and down her neck to her collarbone. He caressed her breast through the thin warmup. "You're not wearing a bra."

"I dressed in a hurry." She pulled his hand against her breast again, hungry for the feel of him. She wanted his touch everywhere on her body.

He slid the zipper on her shirt down, following with a trail of kisses that ended between her breasts. Then he insinuated his hand inside the shirt and eased the fabric aside, bringing her breast out into the light.

He pushed her up against the Sub-Zero fridge and kissed her breast, first with reverence, then with an increasing hunger. As he suckled, flames of hot desire shot from her breast through her body to the very core of her, and the heat made her whimper with need.

He peeled off her shirt and then his, fumbling with the buttons in his haste, getting his hand caught in the cuff, tugging until buttons flew off. He pressed his bare chest against hers and groaned.

"Oh, yes." The hair on his chest abraded her sensitive nipples, sending more of those white-hot flames licking through her, making her squirm.

"Lucy, we have to stop."

"Oh, no. No, no, no, don't do this to me."

"We don't have any birth control."

"We don't need it. I have the implant."

"Seriously?"

She went to work on his linen suit pants. "I wouldn't joke about something like that. Now, make love to me, Bryan Elliott, or that pot of chocolate sauce is going over your head."

Seven

Bryan had always been a man who used his good judgment in all decisions, but he was beyond judgment now. Lucy Miller had just removed the last barrier to their making love. No unforeseen consequences could result from their intimacy.

He kissed her again, inhaling her. She smelled even better than the chocolate, which would have been a poor substitute for indulging in Lucy.

"I should take you up to bed," he whispered.

"No. You'll change your mind if I give you even half a chance."

"Or you will." He slid both hands inside the stretchy waist of her warmup pants. She wore only the briefest of thongs under them, which meant her cheeks were bare. He filled his hands with her rounded bottom while he continued kissing her, rubbing up against her small but perfect breasts. Her nipples were hard as glass beads against his chest, and they burned him like a brand.

She managed to get his pants unfastened and her own hands were as busy as his. She thrust them inside his boxers, groaning as one hand found his arousal.

"Whoa, Lucy." He had to distract her or he was going to go off like a defective bottle rocket. He couldn't recall the last time he was this turned on, possibly never. But he felt as if the foreplay had been going on all evening. Every look she gave him, every innocent or not-so-innocent touch, had led to this.

He pulled her pants and thong down past her knees in one fluid movement. She gasped in surprise, but she was about to get an even bigger surprise. He leaned down, placed a shoulder against her waist, wrapped his arms around her thighs, and picked her up in a fireman's carry.

She squealed in protest. "Bryan, what are you doing? Put me down." She reached out and slapped at his rear, but it was hardly more than a tap.

He retaliated with a slightly smarter smack to her bare bottom. "Behave."

"Ow!" She laughed. "What are you doing?"

He carried her only as far as the large counter where the chefs assembled the plates of food just before the wait staff whisked them out to their patrons. "You think you're the only one who's allowed to do something outrageous? You think you're the only one who can seduce?"

"Oh, Bryan, I didn't set out to seduce you. Not really." She wrapped her hands around his head, pressing his face against her breasts, and he didn't protest. He was in heaven.

"I was worried about you. You'd been gone so long.

If you hadn't had the whipped cream on your face, this never would have happened."

"Well, it did, missy. You started it and I'm going to finish it." He leaned against her, pushing her until she lay with her back on the counter. Then he stripped her pants and underwear all the way off her feet, pulling off her running shoes in the process. They dropped with a clunk to the floor, and he pulled her knees apart and stepped between her thighs.

She quivered with anticipation, and he had to admit it would have been easy just to drop his own pants and bury himself in her. He tested her readiness with one finger and felt that she was slick.

She gasped at his featherlight touch.

"Please," she said. "Do it now."

Not before he'd tasted her. With his own stomach knotted in anticipation, he leaned down and, using his fingers to open her, lightly grazed her with a flick of his tongue.

She wiggled and moaned again. "Oh, no, please, no more…"

"Maybe you'll think twice before you do that trick with the chocolate sauce again," he said with a low growl before tasting her once more. He held her hips firmly so she couldn't wiggle right out of his reach, and he tasted her yet again, drinking more deeply this time, letting his tongue explore.

Lucy reached out and grabbed a handful of his hair. "Bryan!"

He did not take pity on her. He waited until he sensed she was verging on the peak of pleasure. Then he raised up, shed his own garments, slid her hips to the edge of the counter and plunged himself into her warmth.

"Oh!" Lucy cried out. "I can't— Oh, my—"

Bryan thrust again, more deeply this time, and again until he was buried to the hilt. She was tight and warm and slick and he was going to lose control of himself. It was too much.

He felt Lucy's spasms of ecstasy just before she cried out one last time. Three more hard thrusts, and it was over for him, too, but he'd known he wouldn't last long inside Lucy. Not with the buildup he'd had over the past hours—hell, the past days.

Lucy sat up suddenly and, still joined to him, threw her arms around him and kissed him. She clung sweetly to him and rubbed her face against his hair.

"Please don't leave me, don't ever leave me," she said. "I want to be together like this forever."

He thought about telling her how awkward it would be for the chefs to work around them when they came to work tomorrow, but he held his tongue. This wasn't a moment for humor.

Lucy might seem strong, but in many ways she was fragile, and he had to remember that. She might have been a bit brazen tonight, but he knew she didn't take this sort of thing casually.

He tried not to take her plea about never leaving too seriously. People said all kinds of strange things during a sexual climax. Refined ladies cursed like sailors, and sailors wept like children.

He hoped she didn't mean anything by it. Because he would leave her eventually. No matter how much he didn't want to.

He gently separated himself from her, wrapped his arms around her and slid her off the counter and onto legs that wobbled slightly before she found her balance.

"You okay?" He smoothed her hair out of her face.

"I think I'll live."

"Ready to put your clothes on and go upstairs?"

"You aren't seriously asking me to go upstairs without eating some of that cake, are you?"

Funny, he'd forgotten all about the cake. "Let's take it with us. We can eat it in bed."

She grinned, pushed him farther away from her and retrieved her discarded clothes. "Last one dressed has to spread whipped cream all over the other one and lick it off."

That was one contest Bryan wouldn't mind losing—though winning sounded pretty good, too.

Lucy had sobered by the time they got upstairs, fully dressed and carrying two plates of cake plus the rest of the dessert, which Bryan had sealed into a Tupperware cake plate.

Her face grew warm as she recalled how wanton she'd been—and then how she'd clung to Bryan, pleading with him not to leave.

She hadn't meant to do that last part. She'd still been in the throes of the most intense orgasm of her life, and the words had just poured out of her right past her brain.

She knew she still had some issues about Cruz Tabor. The In Tight drummer had ended the relationship without warning, in the cruelest of fashions, and now she had a sort of phobia about being abandoned.

But such pleas would be useless where Bryan was concerned. Their relationship could not be anything but temporary. He'd given her fair warning—unlike that bastard Cruz, who'd led her to believe he was crazy in love with her and that he would marry her someday.

She would just make things worse if she clung to Bryan. She had to adopt the mindset that every day they had together was a gift, and that when they inevitably parted ways, she would have some incredible memories and, hopefully, no hard feelings.

Hell, she wasn't even sure Bryan wanted to have a relationship, temporary or otherwise. She'd pushed him into sex, and men were pretty helpless to say no when sex was offered.

She chanced a glance at him as the elevator reached his loft. He was staring at her.

"What?" she said with a nervous giggle.

"You're just so absolutely gorgeous I can't stop looking at you."

"Oh, yeah, right. In these really sexy clothes, no makeup, glasses, my hair's a wreck—"

"Stop that. You are beautiful, with or without designer clothes and cosmetics. I don't know who told you you weren't, but he was an idiot."

The door opened, and he ushered her ahead of him.

"It wasn't a he. It was my mother. She thought I was going straight to hell when I died anyway, for being willful and lazy and disrespectful. But she said that at least she didn't have to worry about me doing bad things with boys, because God hadn't gifted me in a way that would make any boy take notice."

Lucy had always made light of her mother's criticism, but saying the words aloud after all these years still produced a tightness in her chest.

"That's criminal," Bryan said, his jaw pulsating. "No wonder you don't miss your parents so much."

"Oh, she meant well. She was always so afraid for me—afraid for my soul. She just knew I was headed down the path straight to hell. The sad thing was, I proved her right."

"You?"

"I lived up to her worst fears." And that was all Lucy would say on that subject. "Can we really eat cake in bed?"

"Your mother wouldn't approve."

"My mother would be on her knees for a week, praying for my salvation, if she knew I'd colored my hair. Eating cake in bed with a man would be beyond her comprehension."

"Then I guess we won't worry about what Mom would think."

Lucy took a deep breath and realized, for the first time in a long time, that she didn't feel guilty for enjoying herself, for having fun. Maybe she was making progress.

She nodded toward the stairs. The last of Bryan's anger left his face. He grinned, left the cake in the kitchen, took one of Lucy's plates and her hand and led her upstairs.

"Here's the thing about eating cake in bed, though," he said with mock gravity. "There are rules."

"Such as?"

"You have to do it naked."

"I can do that." She smiled wickedly, set the plates down on the king-size bed and took off her clothes. In less than a minute they were both naked and in bed, feeding each other the decadent dessert without benefit of forks, which they'd forgotten.

"This cake is fabulous. You just made this up tonight?"

Bryan made a production of licking whipped cream

off her fingers. "You inspired me. I needed something so decadent it would distract me from you. I'm going to put it on the menu, and I'm going to call it Lucy's Cake."

"Don't you mean Lindsay's Cake? Everyone would wonder who the heck Lucy was."

"Once we catch our embezzler—and find Stungun—you can go back to using your real name."

"Right." Lucy didn't add that once that happened, there would be no more need for his girlfriend ruse. No more need for her to remain in New York.

Bryan set the two empty plates on the nightstand and slid more deeply under the covers, pulling her with him. "We need to work off a few calories, you know," he said.

"I'm all sticky. Maybe I should take a shower."

"I like you all sticky." To prove his point, he kissed all around her mouth and started doing crazy things with his hands, rubbing her belly and thighs, petting her as if she were a cat.

Lucy wondered if he'd noticed that her belly wasn't quite as flat and firm as it ought to be. Also, anyone who looked closely would see her faint stretch marks.

She reached over and turned off the lamp. Maybe someday she would tell Bryan the truth about her past. But not tonight.

Bryan woke before dawn, and it took him a few seconds to reason why there was a warm female body snuggled up to him. When he remembered, he smiled. He and Lucy had gone completely crazy last night. He'd never have guessed that a mild-mannered little bank employee in a shapeless suit would be such a wildcat in bed. She wasn't just responsive, she was imaginative. He'd believed himself to be fairly experienced and uninhibited, but she'd shown him a few things that had driven him completely wild.

He should have felt guilty for taking Lucy into his bed. She was a witness, a civilian cooperating to bring down a terrorist sympathizer. She'd done everything he'd asked of her, and he'd promised his protection.

But he couldn't muster much guilt. He didn't feel as if he'd taken advantage of her. Though he'd been the one to initiate their first kiss two days before, she'd been the aggressor last night. He'd gone out of his way *not* to seduce her. She'd come to him with her eyes wide open, knowing he was not cut out for a committed relationship.

As for compromising her ability to be a good witness, he didn't see it. As far as anyone would know, she was posing as his girlfriend so he could protect her. No one ever needed to know that the fiction had become reality. He could keep a secret—and apparently Lucy could, too. There were definitely parts of her past she hadn't revealed.

She was entitled to her privacy. Whatever her secrets, he didn't imagine they had any bearing on the case. But he wanted her to trust him.

"You awake?" she whispered.

"Mmm-hmm."

She snuggled closer. "Why? It's not even light out."

"Just thinking. Lucy, you don't have to answer if you don't want, but I'm just curious. I dug around in your past pretty thoroughly, and I didn't find any boyfriends in the past couple of years."

"No, I didn't date anyone after I moved to Virginia."

"Why do you have the implant, then?"

"I'm optimistic?"

"You weren't acting like a woman on the hunt for a lover."

"But I found one. By accident. And isn't it a good thing I'm protected?"

"Yes, of course." He wasn't quite sure why he was so bothered by this scenario. He supposed it was because he was trained to notice inconsistencies. And women with no immediate prospects for sex didn't usually worry about birth control.

"All right, I'll explain it to you," she said. "It's not a pretty episode in my past, and you'll probably be repulsed, but I want to be honest. Your background check missed a few relevant facts about me."

"Those two missing years?"

"Yeah. I wasn't just working for In Tight. I was sort of a…well, a groupie."

"You?"

"I started out just wanting to do my job. I was content to be a very small part of In Tight. I was starstruck, and being close to a rock band was like heaven, especially after my conservative upbringing. Most of the guys knew my name, and they actually talked to me occasionally—usually when they wanted to get paid—and that was fine with me. Then came Cruz Tabor."

"He's in the group, isn't he?"

"The drummer. He started coming on to me—big-time. I was just this nerdy accountant from Kansas, and he made me feel special. We started…well, I guess you wouldn't call it dating. We started sleeping together."

That bastard! Then Bryan tempered his first thought. After all, wasn't he guilty of the same thing? That Tabor guy had fallen victim to Lucy's winsome charms, and who could blame him?

"He treated me pretty well at first," Lucy continued. "We were a couple. I even got my picture in a tabloid once, though I wasn't identified. When the band went on tour, he let me ride with him in first class—they didn't have their own private jet back then."

Bryan wondered how he could have missed all this when he'd dug into Lucy's past. But it sounded as if her activities with In Tight wouldn't have left a paper trail, and he hadn't gone so far as to interview her family or friends. The check had been more routine than that. He'd mostly been concerned with whether she had a criminal record or mental illness.

He lightly rubbed her arm, urging her to continue.

"Things were pretty good, until I got pregnant."

Bryan grew very still. Lucy had been pregnant?

"Cruz had said he loved me, that he wanted to marry me as soon as the band got better established. I thought he'd be happy about the baby. Instead he was horrified. No, that's not the right word. Disgusted. He blamed me for not being more careful, and he told me to…to g-get rid of it." Her voice cracked, and Bryan pulled her more closely against him.

He felt a rage against the insensitive bastard. "If I ever meet this man, I'll yank out his esophagus," Bryan said. "You didn't…" But maybe she had. Clearly she had no child now.

"No, I didn't terminate the pregnancy. I told Cruz I thought he was horrid and that I was having the baby. He said he would deny it was his and claim I was a slut and I slept around with everyone."

Bryan's anger escalated toward boiling. "DNA could have proved—"

"I didn't want that man acknowledged as my child's

father. Not after the way he acted. He knew I could prove he was the father, and he offered me money to just go away. But I didn't take it. I just left."

"So, what happened?" Bryan asked, though he was afraid he knew.

"I went home to the farm. My parents were scandalized, of course. They dragged me to church a lot and prayed for me. But I was their daughter, and eventually they forgave me. Then I lost the baby."

"Oh, Lucy, I'm sorry."

"The strange thing was, I really wanted her. Everyone said losing her was a blessing, but I didn't agree, and I felt so guilty, like I was being punished. I should have listened to my parents. I shouldn't have been so wild. Taking risks for myself was one thing, but my foolhardy behavior had created a human being. It sobered me. To make amends, I swore I would never, ever take any kind of risk, ever again. I would work at the job my uncle found for me, I wouldn't call attention to myself, I would be humble."

"And the implant?"

"I'm weak," she said. "I wouldn't go looking for trouble, but what if trouble found me? I wanted to be ready, just in case. I wouldn't, couldn't, take a chance on another unplanned pregnancy. And was I right? Yes. Trouble found me. And I have no ability to resist temptation, as I've so amply illustrated tonight."

"You're not weak," he said. "You're one of the strongest women I've ever met. You made a mistake—you fell in love with the wrong man, that's all. It happens every day."

"But who's to say it won't happen again? To me?"

He understood exactly what she was saying. He was

the wrong man for her. Another bad choice. "I would never turn my back on my own child," he said.

"I know. You're not anything like Cruz. He was a self-absorbed, spoiled child. You're responsible and mature."

"You can say that with a straight face after everything we did last night?" He almost blushed thinking about what they'd done in the restaurant kitchen.

"Yes, I can. I know you would put my life before yours in a heartbeat. But I also know that you would not choose to have a baby. Fortunately, that's not something you have to worry about."

He shifted his weight on top of her and kissed her, filled with a rush of affection for her. She'd made some difficult decisions. She'd taken responsibility for her actions.

He wished he could be the right man for her. She deserved someone who would love her unconditionally. Someone who would be there for her, always, not running off on dangerous missions, staying gone for weeks at a time. Someone who would welcome her babies.

Yes, she was right about him. He would not choose to bring a child into the world—for all the same reasons he chose not to marry or let his professional and personal lives become enmeshed. He refused to put his loved ones in danger or make them worry about him.

"I guess I didn't repulse you?" she asked.

"Nothing you could do would repulse me." On the contrary, everything she said and did turned him on more. She was like an addictive drug.

"Good. Because I was rather enjoying all this." She reached down, running her hand along his ribs, then across his chest. Her fingers paused to explore the raised scar that ran along his sternum.

"You'll find lots more of those on me if you look," he said. "I've got a dandy one on my leg, another across my back. I'm not very pretty."

She huffed at that, then skittered across his belly with her hand, arriving at his growing arousal. "This is all the pretty I need." She took it possessively into her hand.

He groaned.

"I know it's temporary," she said.

"It'll last long enough."

She giggled. "No. I meant you and me. I know we can't be together long-term. But I'm okay with that. I don't want you to feel bad."

"I don't feel bad. I feel very, very good, and I'm going to feel better in a moment or two." He moved on top of her. He did not want to talk about, or even think about, the day they would say goodbye.

Lucy stood under the spray in Bryan's enormous shower, feeling cleansed both inside and out. She was glad she'd unburdened herself last night. Maybe her confession was a bit more elaborate than Bryan had been prepared for, but she'd needed to say it. She hadn't talked about Cruz or her pregnancy to anyone since her miscarriage. Her parents had wanted her to bury the past, forget it had ever happened. But as awful as it was, Cruz and the pregnancy were a part of her now. She felt she had a new perspective on it. Yes, she'd been naive, and she'd made a mistake. But she wasn't evil.

Thanks to Bryan, she wasn't stuck anymore. She could move on, live normally, leave the sackcloth and ashes behind.

Bryan tapped on the bathroom door. "You're going to use up all the hot water."

He was back from cleaning up the restaurant. "Then join me." She'd been fantasizing about herself and Bryan in this decadent shower, with its acres of red glass tile and twin shower sprays, since she'd first seen it the day Scarlet came over for her makeover.

"Hey. You don't have to ask me twice."

Just when she thought she couldn't possibly make love again, for she ached in places she hadn't known existed, they did.

Eight

Lucy had mixed feelings about her computer work now. Yes, she wanted to solve the puzzle of who the embezzler was at Alliance Trust. But the sooner that person was arrested and all parties brought to justice, the sooner she and Bryan would part.

Duty won out, and she worked hard on her latest project, which was matching up log-in times with the times the illicit funds transfers had occurred.

By lunch, she'd eliminated several more candidates. She was closing in. Only five suspects. One of them was Omar Kalif, a loan officer of Iranian descent. She'd always liked Omar. He was funny and hardworking, and he would turn himself inside out to find a way to get a client qualified for a loan. He had a darling wife, two kids…

Well, she would let Bryan worry about that. Her job was to solve the puzzle.

Bryan had told her he would be tied up today and probably wouldn't be home until late. He'd been vague about what he would be doing. She didn't know if he was in the city or had jetted off some place, risking life and limb.

She tried not to think about it. She tried not to worry, to keep herself busy. But she had a vivid imagination. If anything ever happened to Bryan, would she be notified? What about his family? Would anyone explain to them that he was a spy, that he'd died defending their country? Or would he just disappear, leaving the family to wonder?

She couldn't live like that long-term. Even if Bryan were willing to change his policy and make a commitment, she didn't think she could. Yes, it was exciting working with and living with a spy. But it wasn't a forever kind of arrangement.

Bryan had told her to go downstairs to the restaurant when she got hungry, that Stash would take care of her. He'd fixed the elevator so it would recognize her voice and had instructed her on passwords and "panic passwords"—in case she was ever in the elevator under duress. She'd laughed at the cloak-and-dagger antics, but he'd been serious.

She went down to Une Nuit to rustle up some lunch. She entered through the kitchen, and her face grew warm as she was reminded of what had gone on there the previous night.

"Lindsay!" Stash Martin greeted her with a double air-kiss. "Bryan said you'd be down for lunch. Scarlet's in the Elliott booth if you want to sit with her."

"I don't want to intrude—"

"Nonsense. I am sure she would welcome your

charming company." Refusing to acknowledge any further protests, Stash led her into the dining room, where Scarlet, dressed in the most gorgeous teal dress with feathers all around the neck, shared a booth with another woman who had her back to Lucy.

Scarlet looked both surprised and pleased when she saw Lucy. "Oh, please join us," she said. "We haven't even ordered yet. This is Jessie. I don't think you've met her."

The other woman smiled warmly and shook Lucy's hand. "Nice to meet you, Lindsay."

"Same here. Scarlet, I didn't realize you had another sister."

"What?" both women said at the same time.

Lindsay looked at Scarlet, then Jessie, then Scarlet again. Though they weren't as similar as Scarlet and Summer, the family resemblance was unmistakable.

"You're sisters, right?"

Scarlet laughed, and Jessie just looked horrified.

"What in the world would make you think that?" Jessie said, a little more strongly than Lucy thought was called for.

"Sorry, I thought I saw a family resemblance," Lucy said, trying to smooth over the awkward moment. "My mistake."

Scarlet explained, "This is Jessie Clayton. She's my intern at *Charisma*."

"You know," Jessie said, "I've really got an awful lot of work to do. I think I'll skip lunch." She tried to slide out of the booth, but Scarlet leaned over and put a hand on her arm to stop her.

"Oh, come on, Jessie, I'm not a slave driver. You can take time for lunch."

"No, really, I have to go." She stood and made good her escape despite both Lucy's and Scarlet's protests.

Lucy sat on the recently vacated leather banquette. "Sorry. I didn't mean to scare her off."

Scarlet looked perplexed. "That was strange. I wonder what got into her? Maybe she was distressed at the idea that she looks like me."

"Oh, yes, you're such an ogre," Lucy said. "No one wants to look like you."

"Do you really think there's a resemblance? Because I thought so, too, when I first hired her, but then I decided I was imagining things."

"Well, lots of people look similar," Lucy said, downplaying the uncanny resemblance. "She's probably got Irish in her, like you."

Scarlet ordered mineral water and her favorite salad Niçoise, which came adorned with tiny eggrolls. Lucy, who continued to be delighted by the French/Asian blended menu, ordered an egg-drop soup Florentine.

"That's all you're having?" Scarlet asked.

"After that huge dinner last night, I haven't been very hungry." Not to mention the orange-chocolate-mint cake.

"So where's Bryan today?"

"Out and about. I'm not sure."

"So he doesn't tell you any more about his business than he tells anyone else?"

"I don't want to be nosy."

"Well, I am. Honestly, the whole family is a little fed up with him. He's been so secretive lately. We all thought maybe you were the secret, but apparently not, since he's still doing his disappearing act."

"He'll be back tonight," Lucy said, trying to mask her reaction. She wondered if Bryan knew just how worried his family had become about him. That was something he'd tried to avoid at all costs.

Scarlet asked about Lucy's clothes, how everything was working out and whether she needed anything else. "We're doing a shoot tomorrow with the most gorgeous Givenchy eveningwear. One of the dresses would look perfect on you. Hey, maybe you could model it. We pay well."

Lucy laughed. That was all she needed, her picture in a national magazine. She might as well send a map to the embezzler with a dotted line leading straight to her.

"No, I don't think so. I have work to do."

"Oh, your novel! I'm so glad you decided to give it another try. How's it going? I know an agent at William Morris. I could probably get you a read."

"I'm a long way from having anything to show." And, boy, wasn't that the truth. "But thank you. You're awfully nice to me."

"That's because I want you to stick around. Bryan clearly needs you in his life. I don't think I've ever seen him quite as happy as he was last night. He couldn't stop staring at you."

Lucy blushed. She wanted to reassure Scarlet that she would stick around. But, of course, she wouldn't.

"Scarlet, hi!" A striking woman with the brightest red hair Lucy had ever seen stopped at their table. Scarlet stood to give the other woman a hug. The redhead towered over Scarlet, no easy feat. She had to be well over six feet tall. Then Lucy realized her face was familiar. She was a supermodel. She went by Redd.

"Redd," Scarlet said, "this is Lindsay Morgan, Bryan's girlfriend."

Lucy had never quite gotten over her awe of celeb-

rities, even after the Cruz disaster. She babbled something to Redd, who eventually left to find her own table.

"It must be fun, seeing celebrities all the time," she said.

"You'll get used to it."

Lucy only wished she would have the opportunity to
get used to it.

Bryan didn't get home until close to nine that night.
Lucy couldn't help herself. She launched herself into his
arms the moment he got off the elevator.

"Hey, hey," he said, returning her hug, rubbing her
back. "Is something wrong?"

"I was just worried about you."

"Why? I told you I'd be late."

"I know. But I didn't know what you were doing, and
I have a vivid imagination. I saw you getting shot,
stabbed, poisoned—"

"Oh, Lucy." He kissed her tenderly. "I wasn't doing
anything dangerous. Just boring legwork. Checking in
with snitches, trying to get a lead on Stungun. I met
with Siberia."

"Does he know Stungun's true identity?"

"No. Only the head of the agency knows. But he's
going to find out. He's making a case to the director
tomorrow. We've got to find him."

"I've made some progress on my end."

"Really?"

"Do you want something to eat? Stash delivered a
huge dinner. I didn't eat a third of it."

He didn't let her go. "I'm starved, but not for food."

"Hmm. I think you tend to confuse your appetites."
She slid out of his grasp. "Sit. I'll warm up a plate and
explain what I've found."

As she heated up the coq au vin tempura, she told him what her research had led her to that afternoon. And she didn't like it one bit.

"I've eliminated everybody but one person. I've double- and triple-checked, and she is the only one who has been logged in every single time there was an illegal withdrawal."

"She?"

"Peggy Holmes, Mr. Vargov's personal secretary. She's a mild-mannered grandmother who's been working at the bank for more than twenty years. I don't really see how she could be a terrorist sympathizer."

"You'd be surprised. One of her children is married to a man who travels frequently to the Middle East with his business. Nothing wrong with that in itself—"

"You already know that?"

"I've done background checks on everyone at that bank. Now that you've identified Peggy as a viable suspect, I'll zero in on the son-in-law."

"But Peggy Holmes? I just don't see it. Of course, she does enjoy helping others and being of service. She lives to please Mr. Vargov. So maybe if someone approached her, made it sound like she'd be doing a great service…"

"What about Mr. Vargov? As the bank president, he'd be in a position of authority and power. You haven't said much about him. He has relatives in former Soviet republics—"

She shook her head. "It couldn't be him. I was able to eliminate him as a suspect first thing. He was in a meeting during every single transaction."

"Every single one?"

"Well, the first few that I looked at. I stopped checking after I was able to eliminate him." When

Bryan still looked skeptical, she added, "Mr. Vargov does attend a lot of meetings."

"Just for fun, let's see where he was during all of the transactions."

"All of them? There are dozens."

"All of them."

Three hours later Bryan had the answer he was looking for. Mr. Vargov had been in some type of meeting on the bank premises during every single illicit transaction. During the two weeks he was on vacation, not a single withdrawal took place.

"But he wasn't even logged onto the computer during most of the transactions," Lucy objected. "He couldn't have performed those withdrawals without logging in and using a password."

"And how hard do you think it would be to figure out his trusty secretary's password? She probably has it written down someplace."

"But how could he have—"

"On his PDA. Your conference room has wireless capability. He could carry on a conversation, casually tapping on his Palm Pilot as if recording lunch plans, log on to the bank's system using Peggy's password, and move money around. Easy as pie."

"I can't believe I didn't see it. It's so obvious! Oh, but Mr. Vargov is so nice. He's like a father to me. He's always been kind, gave me a job when he didn't know me at all, paid me more than I was worth, gave me a really nice office."

"Think about it. If you were going to raid pension funds, who would you want doing the audits?"

Now Lucy got it. "Someone inexperienced. Underqualified. Stupid."

"You would want to pay that person handsomely, keep them happy. A happy employee is much less likely to rock the boat than a dissatisfied one. But you were too smart for him. And too conscientious to forget what you saw just to hold on to your cushy job."

"It all makes sense now." She swiveled in her chair to face Bryan, who'd been sitting behind her looking over her shoulder. "That has to be the answer."

"We are a good team, you and I," Bryan said with a broad grin. "I never could have figured this out without you." He pulled her into his lap and nuzzled her neck. "What do you say we celebrate?"

She kissed him hungrily. After her long day at the computer, and all her worrying about Bryan, she craved release—and she knew just how to get it.

"You'll never guess who I met today," Lucy said later as they lay in bed. "Redd, the supermodel."

"She comes in a lot. She likes the wasabi pate."

"Don't you love owning a restaurant? I think it would be so fun, like entertaining every day. Making up special dishes for special customers, recommending wine—Well, okay, I'd have to learn about wine. But you must enjoy it."

"I do. I wish I could devote more time to it."

Lucy hesitated, then decided she owed it to Bryan to be honest with him about what she'd heard from his relatives. "Your whole family is worried about you, you know. They've noticed your long absences—and your injuries at your brother's wedding. What was that all about?"

"Car accident."

"That's what your father said, but he didn't believe it." Bryan sighed. "It was actually a car bomb. In France.

I realized something was wrong and got out just before the explosion. No one was seriously hurt, thank God."

Lucy was horrified. The car bomb in Paris? "I read about that in the news. It was blamed on terrorists."

"I was with Stungun, investigating the charity, the one our embezzler is sending his funds to. I must have gotten close to them—but not close enough."

"You're not ever allowed to go back to France, do you understand?" Lucy said fiercely. "My God, someone there tried to kill you!"

He shrugged. "It happens a lot."

"Don't tell me any more. I can't stand it."

"I won't. But you have to reassure my family that everything's fine. Can you do that?"

"No, Bryan, I can't. I can't tell them not to worry when you could get blown up at any time."

"I'm not going to get blown up."

"Someday, some bad guy is going to catch up with you," she said in a small voice.

He kissed her cheek in an achingly tender gesture. "I'm not going anywhere. I promised I wouldn't leave you, didn't I?"

"You'll be gone again tomorrow."

"For a few hours only. I'll be back. We're having a big party at the restaurant. The half-year profit margins have been calculated at EPH, and the company has broken all previous records. Apparently Granddad's little game has produced the desired results."

"Which magazine is winning?"

"*Charisma.* No one's too surprised, the way Aunt Fin's been working her tail off. But there are still six months to go."

"Have you talked to your dad?"

"He doesn't seem to care that *Snap* is in last place. I think he's a little more broken up about his divorce than anyone suspected."

"Well, the breakup of any marriage is traumatic, even a bad marriage," Lucy said pragmatically. "He's got another six months to pull things together. Do you want him to get the CEO spot?"

Bryan shrugged. "I just want him to be happy. He hasn't been happy in a long time."

Lucy was bored out of her mind. Bryan had been gone longer than the "few hours" he'd promised, but she didn't hold it against him. He was working hard to catch the embezzler, which was his job.

But she missed him, and she had no more computer puzzles to distract her. She'd gone about as far as she could with the data she'd downloaded from Alliance Trust. Now it was up to Bryan to confirm the theory they'd come up with.

He didn't give her many details, but she gathered that he was having Mr. Vargov put under surveillance. Such operations were tricky, involving other arms of Homeland Security besides his own. And given that he had to protect his anonymity, even from other operatives, arrangements had to be made through intermediaries and other secure communications, all of which could take time.

Three hours before the EPH party, Bryan's phone rang. Lucy checked the Caller ID and saw the call came from Une Nuit, so she answered happily, thinking Bryan must be back.

Instead, she found Stash Martin on the other end of the line. "Lindsay, I am glad I caught you at home."

Like, where else would she be? "Bryan just called and said he would be delayed. He wants you to finalize the menu for the party tonight."

"Me? Why?"

"He said you have good taste."

"Good taste in men, maybe," she said, which made Stash laugh. "All right, I'll be down in a minute." She was grateful for any distraction, provided her magic key still worked on the elevator. She hadn't asked Bryan about that.

Fifteen minutes later she and Stash were bent over an array of menus, some printed, some handwritten, that had been assembled for various parties over the years. Apparently, the regular menu didn't include even a fraction of what the kitchen could do. Bryan regularly rotated dishes on and off, which kept things interesting for the clientele.

"Stash, you have to help me choose," she said, overwhelmed by the exotic-sounding dishes. "Is there anything that's a particular favorite of the Elliotts? Anything they hate? Do any of them have food allergies?"

"No allergies. One or more of the ladies are always watching their carbs, so you should choose at least one dish with that in mind."

"All right, how about this grilled chicken with the cashew and water chestnut stuffing?"

"Excellent choice. Now, something with a bit more oomph for the adventurous palettes."

"Quiche Cantonese?"

Stash nodded his approval. They went on in this fashion, with Stash giving her hints. Obviously, he could have put together the menu by himself, but Bryan had wanted to let her make the choices, which warmed her heart. He was being very thoughtful. Her choice of wine was strictly a guessing game, but she trusted Stash not to allow her to make a really dumb mistake.

As she showered and began to dress a little while later, she realized she was looking forward to her dinner. She'd enjoyed planning it and couldn't wait to see how the Elliotts reacted to it.

She'd meant it when she told Bryan she thought owning a restaurant would be fun. She'd always enjoyed good food and had been ecstatic to discover dishes beyond the plain meat and potatoes she'd been raised on. She could hold her own in a kitchen. Her mother had taught her the basics, and she'd done some experimenting during her In Tight days, before Cruz had begun taking up all her time and attention. During the past couple of years she hadn't cooked anything too exciting—that would have fallen under the category of indulging herself and having fun, things that had been off her list. But she'd bought cookbooks and read them.

She loved Une Nuit—the whole package. She loved the bustle in the kitchen, the various chefs yelling at each other, sometimes in languages she didn't understand. She loved the smells and sounds, the well-heeled patrons in the dining room, blissfully unaware of the contained panic going on behind closed doors as Chef Chin demanded perfection. She loved the soft jazz music that played in the background, the muffled din of forks and chopsticks and ice tinkling in glasses, the easy laughter as diners reveled in their own senses.

She sighed. It wasn't her world, but she enjoyed being a part of it. This was much better than being on the fringes of the music business, which was glamorous but painfully sordid.

The bedroom door opened, and Lucy gasped and held her skirt in front of her until she realized the intruder was Bryan. He grinned at finding her in her panties and bra.

"You scared me half to death. The least you could do is stomp when you come up the stairs, so I'll have some warning."

"I'd much rather catch you unaware," he said with a devilish glint in his eyes. "Aren't you fetching. C'mere."

She did, and he wrapped his arms around her and kissed her as if he'd been away for weeks instead of hours. Her knees got all wobbly and her chest ached from shortness of breath.

"Sorry I took so long. Did you get everything sorted out with Stash?"

"You didn't ask?"

"I came straight upstairs. Couldn't wait another moment to see you, and thank goodness I didn't delay." He slid one hand inside her panties.

"We don't…uh…really have time to…uh…" She couldn't come up with a more energetic objection. In truth, they could have had an appointment with the Queen of England, and she'd have made the monarch wait.

"We'll just have to be fashionably late."

Bryan had his clothes off in seconds. Rather than take her to the bed, he sat in a cushy chair that was intended for reading, and pulled Lucy into his lap. She didn't need much coaxing; the moment she'd seen him, her body had started preparing itself for him. She was flushed, her nipples hard and aching for his touch, and she was warm deep inside and already tingling between her legs though he'd not yet touched her there.

She wiggled out of her panties, threw her bra aside, all the while making certain to brush against Bryan's arousal as much as possible. When she turned to face him again, she straddled him in the big chair, torturing him unmercifully by brushing her soft curls against him.

"You're teasing me."

"Are you suggesting we rush?" she asked innocently.

From behind, he reached between her legs and slipped a finger inside her. She gasped and whimpered, no longer in a teasing mood. "Okay, let's rush."

"That's my girl," he said as he poised his shaft at her entrance. She lowered herself onto him, letting him slowly fill her, enjoying every inch of him.

Once they were joined, he did manage to take his time, grasping her by her bottom and controlling the depth of his strokes. She braced her hands on his shoulders and, as always, let him have his way with her. Any control she had over him was a myth in her own mind.

She let her body take over, her mind just along for the ride, until the exquisite pressure released in an explosion of tingly heat and tremors that reverberated all the way to her fingers, toes and eyelashes.

Bryan let go as the last of her cries of passion echoed across the bedroom. She fell on top of him, too weak to sit up straight, and felt his body convulse as he emptied himself inside her.

They didn't move for a couple of minutes until Bryan finally broke the silence. "I love watching you come."

"Ditto."

"You don't hold back anything. It's all in your face to see—every emotion is all right there."

She sincerely hoped not—because she feared she

was falling in love with Bryan Elliott, and there wasn't a damn thing she could do to stop it except walk away.

And that cure was worse than the disease.

Nine

They were ten minutes late for the party in the private dining room on the floor below the restaurant, but no one seemed to notice or care. The first appetizers were being passed around, wine was flowing and conversation hummed.

Bryan noticed that someone had put place cards on the table. "Was this your idea?" he said, picking up his own and showing it to Lucy.

She nodded. "I thought it might be better if everyone from the same magazine didn't sit together. So we don't have conversational cliques."

And Lucy had done something else rather bold: instead of putting together two long tables, she'd arranged the copper-top tables into a big square.

"Is it okay?" she asked uncertainly. "I thought everyone would be able to see and talk to everyone else this way."

"You think my family needs to talk more?"

"They talk a lot. Just sometimes not in the most productive ways. And some of them could do with more listening."

Bryan laughed. "I hope you're not fantasizing you can be a peacemaker. The bitching and moaning and yelling isn't going to stop until someone is named CEO."

"I can try."

Stash appeared to take drink orders, but everyone seemed content with the wine.

"Do you want to check the menu?" he whispered to Bryan.

"I'm sure it's fine. But I don't see any garlic butter."

"I'll send someone down."

"I'll come up and get it. I want to make the rounds in the dining room."

Upstairs, he did some glad-handing. He sent a bottle of wine to a man he recognized as a competing restaurateur, comped a plate of hors d'oeuvres to several cast members from a soap, paid his respects to an opera diva.

Then he spotted someone he hadn't seen in his rounds, a woman dining alone at a small table, nursing a glass of red wine. Her eyes darted around the dining room until finally her gaze found him, and she smiled uncertainly.

He walked briskly to her table, and she stood to greet him.

"Mom. Why didn't you tell me you were coming? How come no one told me you were here?"

Amanda Elliott hugged her son, then straightened her neat suit jacket. "I'm not sure your new hostess recognized me. And if you're busy, it's okay."

"Never too busy for you. Mom, there's someone I'd like you to meet. She's downstairs." He hesitated, knowing his mother was no longer comfortable around the Elliott clan. "We're having a party to celebrate EPH profits."

"Then you're busy. I'll come back—"

"No, Mom, I think you should join us. Karen's here." His aunt Karen was the one Elliott Amanda had remained close to, other than her sons.

"Is Patrick here?" she asked warily.

"He meant to be, so he could whip everyone into a frenzy of competition. But he canceled. Gram's not feeling well, and he didn't want to leave her home alone."

Amanda immediately showed her concern. "Maeve's all right, isn't she?"

"Just her arthritis acting up. Come on, bring your wineglass. Everyone will be happy to see you."

"Everyone? Then your father's not here?"

"Everyone, and he is here. His divorce from Sharon is final, you know."

"I heard. I also heard about your new girlfriend, and I am curious."

Bryan took his mother's arm, giving her no chance to protest further. He forgot about the garlic butter that had sent him upstairs in the first place.

"Everyone, look who I found."

Amanda looked embarrassed, but Bryan wasn't disappointed in his family. Several of his cousins popped out of their chairs to greet Amanda with a hug. They were all fond of her, and her absence at family gatherings was always commented on, except by Patrick.

Then there was Daniel, Bryan's father, who never said anything about Amanda. But Bryan knew his parents still had lingering feelings for each other.

"Mom," Bryan said, "I want you to meet Lindsay Morgan."

"Lindsay." Amanda took both of Lucy's hands in hers. Bryan was alarmed by the sheen of tears in his mother's eyes. What was that about? Surely the mere sight of Lucy didn't fill Amanda with despair. She'd never been like some moms, thinking no girl was good enough for her boys.

They exchanged a few pleasantries, and Lucy said, "Oh, Mrs. Elliott, won't you join us?" Without even realizing it, Lucy had slipped into the role of hostess. It seemed a natural for her. What was more, it felt somehow…right.

"Call me Amanda, please. And I can see you all are in the middle of something. Bryan insisted I come down and say hi, but I'll be on my way now." But her turndown lacked conviction. Bryan could tell she wanted to stay. Though she often claimed she'd been much happier away from the big, noisy Elliott clan, Bryan knew she sometimes missed being a part of something larger than herself.

"Oh, nonsense," said Karen, and Bryan could have kissed his aunt. "You come join us."

"You can take Finola's chair," said Bryan's uncle Shane. "Obviously she can't tear herself away from work, not even to gloat that she's in first place."

This comment started a round of arguments, as it had been intended to do. Amanda shrugged and took the last empty chair where Finola's place card sat. Bryan watched his father's face to gauge his reaction. Daniel's gaze hadn't left Amanda since she'd entered the room, and any fool could tell he was anything but indifferent. But he was guarded enough that Bryan, even with all his training in body language, couldn't tell whether

Daniel was pleased or angry to have his ex-wife—his first ex-wife—thrust into his company. They sat only two chairs away from each other, with a table corner between them, so they could easily converse if they wanted.

More appetizers appeared, followed by the soup and salad choices Lucy had made. It would have been hard for her to go wrong—everything on the Une Nuit menu was designed to be mixed and matched. But Bryan was nonetheless pleased with and, yes, proud of the menu Lucy had put together. He told himself it was because he wanted her to appear to be a good match for him, as befitted their cover. But he knew it went deeper than that, which troubled him. He had no business getting so attached to her. Given the progress they were making on the Alliance Trust case, she wouldn't be with him for long.

As various members of his family got up to stretch their legs between courses, a certain amount of musical chairs took place at the table. Bryan found himself seated next to his cousin Liam, one of Uncle Michael and Aunt Karen's sons. Liam was the chief financial officer at EPH, and just before the main course, he'd made a brief speech detailing the profits at each of the four EPH magazines. He'd also read a prepared speech from Patrick congratulating all of his children and grandchildren for rising to the occasion and making the competition a real horse race.

That had produced a few snide comments about what, exactly, Patrick had intended besides increasing profits, but Lucy, of all people, managed to smooth over the outbursts of acrimony and keep the evening on a pleasant note.

"So, Liam, how close is the race?" Bryan asked his

cousin confidentially. "You gave us the raw numbers, but I understand the winner is the magazine that grows the most, percentagewise."

"It's closer than you can imagine," Liam said in a low voice. "But I chose to underplay that. Other than to say that *Charisma* is in first place, I don't want the other editors to know just how close they are. It'll only make them crazier."

"Things are kind of tense, huh?"

"You have no idea. Everyone's on their best behavior tonight, maybe out of consideration for you and Lindsay and some of the others here who aren't directly involved with the magazines. But I'm afraid—really afraid—that this crazy competition of Granddad's is going to create rifts in the family that can never be healed."

"You're talking about Finola?"

"She was already on shaky ground with Granddad. Frankly I was relieved she didn't show tonight. I'm not sure she could have buried the hatchet, even for one evening."

"In one of her brothers' heads, maybe. Well, she's always had something to prove."

Stash and three waiters chose that moment to appear with several of Une Nuit's famously decadent desserts as well as some pistachio sorbet for those with more modest appetites. When serving was completed, he leaned down to whisper something to Bryan.

"Oh. I'll be right up."

He excused himself from the table, but before he went upstairs, he stopped by Lucy's chair. "Any interest in meeting Britney Spears?"

"Really?" Lucy squeaked. "She's here?"

"Having drinks."

Lucy didn't have to be asked twice. He thought it was charming that she was so starstruck, that her unfortunate experience with Cruz Tabor hadn't made her bitter.

Upstairs the bar was packed, but the crowd seemed to part for Bryan. Many of the regulars knew him and nodded, giving curious glances to Lucy, but he didn't want to take time for introductions now.

He found the Britney Spears party at the very epicenter of the crowd. The star stopped midconversation to greet him. He welcomed her warmly to Une Nuit, introduced her to Lucy, who managed to squeak out a nervous greeting. He ordered a bottle of Cristal on the house, handed Britney a card and told her to call him or Stash if she ever needed anything. He was about to leave when the flash of a camera caught his attention.

The first thing Bryan did was step between Lucy and the camera, which he couldn't see, but he knew the direction it had come from. He didn't relish having his own picture taken and usually managed to avoid it, since celebrity wasn't exactly good for the anonymity required of an undercover operative. But better his face in a tabloid's than Lucy's.

With the second flash, he saw the perpetrator, a tall, skinny kid with frizzy hair and a pocket camera.

Bryan reached him in an instant, grabbed his arm and prevented him from taking another shot. "That's not allowed in here." He walked the kid to the front door.

"You're throwing me out?" he said in a loud enough voice to garner attention.

"No. You give your camera to our hostess for safekeeping. She'll give it back when you're ready to leave."

"Forget it, man," the guy said, jerking his arm out of Bryan's grasp and huffing out the door.

Bryan made a quick apology to Britney, who was gracious about it, and he and Lucy returned to the private party downstairs.

"That was cool," Lucy said. "Thanks. You must think I'm silly."

"No," he said, but he was too preoccupied to say more. Should he have followed that kid, taken the camera away? He wasn't one of the known paparazzi. Probably just a Britney fan. Still, fans sometimes sold their pictures to the tabloids.

Well, nothing he could do about it now.

The next morning, on the way home from their morning run, Bryan stopped at a newsstand and bought the latest issue of *Global News Roundup,* one of the tackiest tabloids on the market. Rather than celebrity news, the *Roundup* sported doctored photos of the president with his supposed alien baby, a giant squid the size of the Queen Mary, and stories about how the government was practicing mind control through chlorinated tap water.

"Not your usual reading material," Lucy commented as Bryan paid the vendor a couple of bucks.

"I have my reasons."

"Surely no paparazzi would stoop to publishing Britney's picture in that rag."

Bryan laughed. "No, I'm not worried about that."

He didn't explain further until they were home, showered, and had shared a breakfast of yogurt and whole-wheat bagels. She'd been pleased to discover Bryan didn't always indulge in the high-fat fare from Une Nuit.

When the dishes were washed and put away, Bryan opened the briefcase he'd taken with him yesterday and produced a thick stack of *Global News Roundup,* to which he added the current issue.

"I have to leave again today."

Lucy groaned. "I know your work is important, but I'm getting a little stir-crazy, stuck in your apartment all day by myself."

"Our surveillance of Vargov has produced some results. He made contact yesterday with a known terrorist sympathizer. Their conversation was encrypted, but the lab is working on it. We think it might lead us to Stungun. If it does, we'll have all the evidence we need to make arrests."

Lucy knew she should be excited to hear that news. She would be out of danger; she could resume her normal life—whatever that was. She could call her parents, who by now might have started to wonder where she was, if they'd tried to call her.

But Bryan's news brought her no joy. "So is this supposed to keep me entertained while you're away?" she asked, ruffling the stack of tabloids. If he thought stories of mutant three-headed dogs and monkey colonies on Mars would be her choice of entertainment, he didn't know her very well.

"In a way, yes. You're good at puzzles, and I've got one for you."

Lucy's interest ratcheted up a notch. "Yeah?"

"The publisher of this rag is a suspected spy. We believe he's supplying information to—oh, let's just say governments unfriendly to the United States— through secret drop sites. And the locations for those drop sites are encoded and published somewhere in his magazine. Our code breakers are working on it and I thought you might like to take a crack."

Lucy was unabashedly thrilled at the idea. "How could I possibly do better than professional code breakers?"

"They're good at encryption, but their training puts limits on them, too. Because you aren't trained, you can think outside the box. Just have a go."

"Okay. But I'll still miss you."

"I'll try and get back soon." He gave her a kiss that ensured she would think of him often during the day, and then he was gone.

Lucy spread the tabloids out on the living room floor—there were eight weeks' worth. She had to figure out what was common to all the issues. For instance, could the encoded information always be hidden in an alien story? Or a story by a certain reporter?

None of her initial ideas worked out, but she kept trying, reading every story, hoping something would jump out at her.

Bryan couldn't have chosen a better way to distract her. She really did love puzzles. She'd invented her own secret code in sixth grade, which she and some of her friends used as the basis for an exclusive club.

She filled legal pads with scribbles, combining and recombining words and phrases. She'd briefly thought maybe the Lucky Lotto numbers were the key, making references to page numbers, column numbers, column inches, but nothing panned out.

Finally she got the idea to look at the ads. There was one ad for a weight-loss product that caught her attention. It ran in all eight issues, and though the graphics looked similar each time, the text in each one was radically different. The advertising copy seemed odd to her— and not totally persuasive. No pseudoscientific jargon, no claims of pounds melting away while you sleep.

She did a web search for the product. She found a badly designed Web site and some discussions on a dieting listserve in which people were puzzled because the product was always out of stock. Yet the ads kept running....

Positive she was onto something, Lucy kept at it. When Bryan returned later that afternoon, she had covered every surface of his living room with yellow paper and sticky notes.

"Bryan!" She jumped to her feet, then almost fell over as her legs cramped from too many hours of sitting on the floor. She realized she was starving too, and was shocked to see the time. She'd forgotten to eat.

"Did you make any arrests?" she asked, not too sure she wanted to hear the answer.

"Not yet. Vargov knows we've got him, though. He went on the run."

"Oh, no."

"We know where he is, but he thinks he's slipped the noose. We're just waiting to see where he goes for help, who he contacts. It shouldn't be much longer." He took his first good look at his living room. "What in the world have you been doing?"

"Breaking a code."

"Any progress?"

"I know this sounds crazy, but I think I've figured it out."

"Ha! I knew you could do it."

Unable to contain her excitement, she showed Bryan how the coded copy referred to a URL connected to the product Web site. On a page of customer testimonials, a matrix of numbers and letters specified streets and block numbers in and around New York.

"You take my breath away," Bryan said. "This is brilliant."

But suddenly all Lucy could think about was taking Bryan's breath away by another method, one that involved a lot less clothing.

Bryan obviously had the same idea, and they didn't even make it to the bedroom. They didn't make it past the living room floor. They rolled naked on the soft, lamb's wool rug, and when their fevered lovemaking was concluded, they both had multicolored Post-it notes stuck to their bodies and in their hair.

A few days later Bryan came home in a foul mood from another of his mysterious errands. It was the first time Lucy had seen him anything but perfectly controlled—well, except for when they were making love—and her heart just about stopped when he rebuffed her normally affectionate greeting.

He was getting tired of her already, she realized. They'd spent too much time together.

He did not volunteer any information about his day, and she didn't ask. She wasn't entitled to the details of his investigation, after all, and she was frankly surprised he'd told her as much as he had over the past few days.

"Scarlet has tickets to a play," she ventured, thinking he might need a diversion. "She invited us to come along with her and John."

"You go ahead if you want. I'm waiting for phone calls."

Lucy knew perfectly well he could receive phone calls anywhere. He didn't need to stay home for that. But she let it pass.

"Then I won't go, either," she declared. "It wouldn't be any fun without— Bryan, what's wrong? Has something happened?"

"Stungun's dead. They found him in the Potomac River."

"That's terrible. I'm so sorry."

"He's been dead for at least a week."

"Which means he didn't disappear because he was on the run. He was murdered."

"Someone killed him, yes. His body wasn't meant to be found. They wanted me to believe he was the betrayer. Now I have no idea who it is. But the list of suspects is shrinking."

He didn't seem to want comforting, so Lucy didn't try to touch him. "I'm so sorry," she said again. "Were you close to him?"

"We don't make friends at the agency. But he was a good man. I didn't want to believe he was dirty. Part of me is relieved that he probably wasn't. But that doesn't do him much good in his condition."

"His family will know he died a hero. Does he have a family?"

"I have no idea. We never exchange personal information."

Lucy wondered whether poor Stungun had a mother, a wife, kids who would mourn him or maybe think he'd run out on them. Would they ever know what happened? Or would he just never come home?

"What if something happened to you?" Lucy asked in a quiet voice. "Would your family know?"

"I have a safety deposit box that will be opened in the event I disappear or die, explaining everything to my family. Well, as much as I can explain."

"I'm not sure I want to talk about this anymore. It's too depressing." A few days ago she'd been so excited about solving the code in the tabloid. She'd been giddy at the idea that her information might help catch a spy and prevent sensitive information from getting into the wrong hands. Now the whole spy thing left her sick to her stomach. It wasn't glamorous. It was dangerous and ultimately tragic.

"There's more bad news," Bryan said. "Vargov got away. He went into a crowd and lost his tail."

Lucy hadn't believed she could feel any lower, but now she did. Even the realization that she wouldn't be leaving Bryan's protective custody anytime soon didn't cheer her. This was no way to live, scared to go out in public, feeling powerless, no job, no home of her own.

They had to catch Vargov and his accomplice. "Do you have a plan?"

"I'm working on it." He took a deep breath, then looked at Lucy and managed a smile. "I'm sorry. I feel like I've really messed things up for you."

"I don't know what you could have done. Who was tailing Vargov?"

"What?"

"Isn't it possible someone let him go on purpose?"

He shook his head. "We recruited some FBI agents on that detail. They couldn't possibly be involved."

Lucy didn't know what else to say on the subject. "Are you hungry?" she asked.

He seemed to have to think about that. "Yeah. I don't think I've eaten all day. Let's go downstairs. The restaurant is quiet this time of day."

Lucy wasn't hungry, but she wanted to keep him company.

Stash put them in the booth reserved for the Elliotts, the most private spot in the whole restaurant. Bryan requested a bowl of Irish stew, though it was hot as blazes outside.

"Surely that's not on the menu," she said, since Irish stew was neither French nor Asian.

"Comfort food. Chef Chin can make anything. Gram used to make that for me."

Poor Bryan. She'd never seen him in such a state. She wanted to make it better, but she couldn't. So she remained silent, sipping on a cup of coffee. She'd be there for him if he wanted to talk.

He ate his meal in silence, too. She doubted he even tasted it—his thoughts seemed to be far, far away.

Stash wandered by and, seeing that Bryan's bowl was empty, asked, "You want some dessert? Chef Chin was experimenting with some lemon-butter fortune cookies this afternoon. I thought they were *magnifique.*"

"Sure," Bryan said absently. Stash headed for the kitchen, but his cell phone rang and he stopped midstride to answer. Bryan watched him, and the ghost of a smile crossed his face. "Ah, I know that look. Stash has a new girlfriend. Those cookies are long forgotten."

"I'll get them," Lucy said, scooting out of the booth.

"Lucy, you don't have to wait on me."

"I don't mind. Sit tight."

Lucy wandered into the kitchen, which was strangely deserted. Now, she thought, where would Chef Chin have stored those cookies? There was a hallway lined with custom shelving where staples were stored in clear plastic storage bins of various sizes. She found something that looked like fortune cookies, opened the container and took a whiff. Lemon. These had to be the ones.

She picked up the container, turned and ran into the chest of a young man wearing the apron of a busboy.

"Oh, excuse—" A hand over her mouth cut off her apology, and the plastic container fell to the floor, cookies spilling and breaking everywhere.

"Shut up," came the urgent voice of the man behind her. "Cooperate, and you won't be hurt."

Oh, right! He wrenched her arms behind her, attempting to handcuff her. Lucy screamed and kicked out viciously at the busboy in front of her. She got in one good blow to the guy's stomach before he captured her legs and quickly wrapped duct tape around her ankles. He performed this task with amazing efficiency, giving the impression that Lucy wasn't his first kidnapping. In seconds flat she was immobilized, gagged and being carried toward the back door.

Ten

Bryan couldn't say exactly what it was that made him follow Lucy to the kitchen. But he felt suddenly uneasy at the idea of Lucy alone and unprotected in a public place. A busboy who had been vacuuming nearby during the lull in business had abruptly abandoned his chore when Lucy passed and had headed too casually in her direction. Bryan followed. He tried to talk himself out of his paranoia. There was no way Vargov or anyone else could know where Lucy was staying. Even his fellow agents had no way of knowing.

Still, he went after her.

When he reached the kitchen, it was oddly deserted. Then he heard a scuffle coming from the pantry hallway, and he didn't think, he just went into action. The gun he kept in an ankle holster somehow made it to his hand as he peered around the corner into the hallway just in time to see two men dressed as busboys heading for the delivery door with Lucy trussed up between them.

"Freeze!" Bryan yelled. They dropped Lucy with a bone-crunching thud. One of them reached into his apron. Bryan wasn't going to give him a chance to show him what was in the pocket. He aimed and shot. The busboy swiveled in time to avoid a fatal shot; he took a bullet in the shoulder and was gone, the other man ahead of him.

Bryan gave chase as far as the alley, but they'd disappeared by the time he cleared the door. He longed to chase them, run them down, demand to know who'd sent them—and how they'd known where to find Lucy. But his concern right now had to be for Lucy. He didn't know whether she was injured or how seriously. She'd been clearly conscious, and he'd seen no visible blood, but other injuries were possible. He returned to her at once. "Don't try to move, Lindsay," he said, amazed he could keep her cover even in the midst of this mess. "You might be injured." He gently pulled off the tape that had been slapped over her mouth.

She struggled to breathe, and Bryan feared the worst. Spinal injury? Broken ribs, punctured lung? But then she managed to gasp in a bit of air.

"I'm…okay."

"You don't look okay." He gave her a smile and brushed the hair back from her face. "Don't try to move, okay?"

Stash appeared in the hallway looking frantic. "What the hell just happened? I found Kim and two of the sous chefs locked in the freezer!"

"Attempted robbery gone bad, I think," Bryan said innocently.

"I…wouldn't cooperate," Lucy said. "They wanted

to kidnap me. My father has money." She pushed up on her elbows despite Bryan's attempt to get her to lie still. "I'm okay, just got the wind knocked out of me."

Bryan was amazed she'd come up with a cover story so quickly.

"Did I hear a shot?" Stash asked. Chef Chin, the other chefs and a couple of waiters had gathered to stare, mouths open in amazement.

"That was just the door slamming," Bryan fibbed. He had reholstered his gun before anyone saw it.

"We should call the police," one of the chefs said.

Bryan supposed there was no way around it. It would look odd if he didn't want to bring in the cops. They'd all gotten a good look at the "busboys," who apparently were new hires just the day before. That in itself wasn't unusual; restaurant staff came and went quickly.

Bryan could have easily picked the handcuff lock and freed Lucy's hands, but that might have invited speculation, too. So he waited for the cops to arrive, and one of them had a handcuff key. An evidence technician collected the duct tape, hoping to find prints.

Blessedly, none of the restaurant patrons ever knew anything was wrong. Only a few tables were occupied, it being way too early for the dinner crowd. The cops conducted their interviews in Bryan's office even as the kitchen was being restored to normal.

The man Bryan had shot managed to leave no blood behind him, and Bryan wondered if he'd been wearing a bulletproof vest.

It was all over in a couple of hours. Lucy was banged up, but that was all.

"What do we do now?" Lucy asked forlornly the

moment she and Bryan were alone. "That wasn't a random act of violence, was it?"

"No way. Pack a bag. We're getting out of here."

"And going where?"

"I don't know. We can't use any of the agency safe houses. I'll figure something out, though."

Lucy did as she was asked without question, disappearing into her bedroom to pack up her few belongings. When she reappeared, pale but looking determined, Bryan thought his heart would break for her. He'd almost lost her. If Vargov had gotten his hands on her, Bryan was a hundred percent sure he'd have killed her. He probably knew she'd stolen data. He had no way of knowing she'd already analyzed the data and implicated him, though he must suspect it.

"We're taking Stash's car," he said. "I told Stash you were upset and I was taking you away for a couple of days, and that my car was in the shop." Stash, always the loyal friend, hadn't even questioned Bryan's story. He'd give Bryan the shirt off his back if Bryan asked.

Minutes later they were on the road in Stash's Peugeot. Rush hour was in full flower, and the stop-and-go traffic was making Bryan crazy. It was impossible to tell whether anyone was following under these circumstances.

"How did they find me?" Lucy asked.

"You haven't called anyone, have you? E-mailed?"

"No, I promise, I haven't contacted anyone. I would tell you if I had. What about that picture from the restaurant?" she asked.

"I monitored all the tabloids, any paper that might publish bad celebrity photos. Nothing."

"What about Web sites? There are a number of fan

sites where amateur photos are welcome. I'm ashamed to admit I used to cruise them all the time."

"Hell, I never even thought of that. But what are the chances that some terrorist would be cruising celebrity fan sites?"

"You'd be surprised. Millions of people search for Britney on the Web every day. Just picture it. Some underling has the tedious job of surveilling my town house in Arlington, waiting for me to come home. He's bored, he's cruising the Web on his cell phone looking for dirty pictures, and there I am."

Bryan agreed that was how it could have happened. "If I ever see that little punk with the camera, I'm going to rip out his esophagus."

"That seems to be a favorite fantasy of yours."

"Oh, that's nowhere near my favorite." He reached over and squeezed her hand. "I know I've said it before, Lucy, but you absolutely amaze me. You held it together really well, protecting my cover even when you'd barely escaped with your life."

"You've kept your superhero identity a secret from your family for a long time. Who am I to ruin it?"

"It's gotten a lot harder, keeping it a secret," he said. "But every time I think about telling them, I imagine my mother's reaction. Or Gram's. They would completely freak out, and I'd have to quit. I'm not ready to quit."

"When you find work you love, I imagine it's hard to give it up."

"You imagine?"

"I haven't found mine yet. Clearly it's not auditing pension funds or managing a rock group's money."

"You'd be good at restaurant management," he said impulsively.

"Oh, I don't know anything about that," she said with a laugh. "I've never even been a waitress."

He didn't argue with her. But he was starting to entertain this fantasy of Lucy working at Une Nuit. She'd be there for him whenever he returned from a mission. Someone he could talk to about his work—at least in general terms. Someone who understood that his work was important and who wouldn't begrudge him the traveling.

But that was a selfish fantasy. He couldn't expect Lucy just to sit at home waiting patiently for him to return, never knowing where he was or what he was doing or whether he was in danger. All of the reasons he'd had for staying unattached still applied.

Once they got away from the city, it was easier for Bryan to determine that no one was following them. He did some basic evasive driving, taking exits at the last minute, pulling U-turns, zig-zagging through residential streets. But no one was tailing them. He stopped to buy gas, casually sweeping the car for tracking devices while the tank filled. Of course he didn't find any; his unseen enemy would have had to anticipate Bryan borrowing Stash's car. But at this point, there was no such thing as paranoia. The bad guys could figure out at any time what car Bryan was driving; by then he wanted to be well away from New York City.

He could take Lucy to a hotel, but hotels required credit cards, of which he had dozens in different names—none of them safe to use. And any hotel that operated on a cash-only basis wasn't some place he wanted Lucy to stay.

Bryan's satellite phone rang. His nerves already on edge, he jumped at the sound of it. He'd always been told that his location could not be traced using this phone, but he suddenly didn't trust anything he'd ever been told by anyone.

"You aren't going to get that?" Lucy asked.

"No." The Caller ID screen was blank—not a good sign.

"So we're totally on our own?"

Bryan didn't know how to answer that. He had the might of the United States Government behind him. But he had to use a certain chain of command, and if he trusted the wrong link in the chain, they were likely both dead.

He decided, though, that he had to trust someone. And if he had to pick only one person, it would be the man currently calling himself Siberia—the man who'd trained him when he'd first moved over to Homeland Security, the man who'd been his mentor. Siberia was not a particularly likable man—his nickname wasn't random. He was cold. But he was smart and capable, and right now, he was the only choice Bryan had.

He dialed the number. "Casanova?" the familiar voice answered on the other end of the line.

"Did you try to call me just now?"

"No. Why?"

"There've been some new developments." He explained to his superior about the photograph, likely published on the Internet, and the kidnapping attempt. "I have to take her someplace safe. But the safe houses that are available aren't safe from our own people—and unfortunately I'm more sure than ever that's where the threat lies."

Siberia was silent for a long time, so long that Bryan feared they'd lost their connection. Finally he spoke again. "There is a place, a new safe house that's just come available. No one in the agency knows of it but me."

"Where is it?"

"In the Catskills. Very isolated. Put Lucy there. Then you and I will put an end to this thing. I have some new intelligence. I believe I know now who our turncoat is. And I know how to catch her *and* Vargov. But it will require us working together."

Her. So Siberia believed the traitor was Orchid. He didn't know what to say. He'd always thought Orchid was solid. She was middle-aged, plain, unremarkable— all the things that made for a forgettable person, which was good for an agent.

"I think someone got to her with romance," Siberia said. "She probably never had a lot of boyfriends. Women are vulnerable that way."

Privately Bryan didn't think women were any more vulnerable than men, whose brains started to misfire the moment a beautiful women entered the room. But he didn't want to argue about it. Presumably Siberia had more to go on than Orchid's gender.

He had a hard time believing Orchid would fall prey to some Romeo terrorist sympathizer. But by the nature of their work, he didn't know her that well, so he couldn't say for sure.

"So where is this little safe house in the woods?" He didn't like it, but he felt he had no choice. He would have to leave Lucy alone, unprotected. But if they could end this thing once and for all, Lucy would finally be safe. And maybe his stomach, which had been twisted in knots for days, could return to normal.

Siberia gave him directions to the cabin in the Catskills, which he memorized. One of his strengths as an agent was his perfect recall. He seldom had to write anything down.

He told Lucy the plan. She didn't seem easy with it, either, but she didn't object. She probably thought he knew best. He wished he thought that was true.

"It'll take two or three hours to get there," he said. He wanted to avoid the toll roads, because often there were cameras at toll plazas. There wasn't much chance their enemy would know what direction they'd gone, but he wasn't taking *any* chances.

The countryside was beautiful, lush and green and dotted with small lakes that shimmered in the setting sun, but Bryan hardly saw it. He kept thinking of the confrontation ahead, and wondering if he would have to kill one of his comrades. And whether he would return to Lucy—or someone else would come for her, breaking the news of his demise.

Now that the shock of Lucy's almost-kidnapping had worn off, she looked tired. A bruise had formed on her cheekbone, and he noticed her reaching up to touch it, to test the soreness. She probably hadn't even known she had the injury until the adrenaline had worn off.

They stopped long before they neared their destination to buy provisions, choosing a crowded chain grocery store in the town of Monticello, where they weren't likely to be noticed or remembered. Bryan included a deli sandwich Lucy could eat in the car. He wasn't hungry, but he'd had the stew earlier. She hadn't eaten since God knew when.

She claimed not to be hungry, either, but she did nibble at the sandwich and sip at a bottle of juice to make him happy.

It was almost nightfall by the time they reached the cabin. Bryan was glad he hadn't had to find it in total darkness. It was up a twisty, narrow mountain road where one false turn could land a car in a ditch—or worse. He'd been relieved to see the cabin when it finally appeared around a bend. It was larger than he expected, well maintained, but old. Probably no air-conditioning or heat.

"It looks nice," Lucy said optimistically. "I've never stayed in a mountain cabin. It'll be like a vacation."

"You should be working on your book."

She grimaced. "Ah, yes. Scarlet offered to put me in touch with a literary agent. What are they going to think when I never write anything? Then again, I won't be here to explain. You'll have to tell them we broke up."

Bryan was sad to say he hadn't even thought that far ahead. "I dread telling the family *that* almost as much as telling them I'm a spy."

"Why's that? I'm sure women have come and gone from your life before."

He shook his head. "My family is absolutely nuts about you. Gram is already planning the wedding. And Cullen— Ever since he found love, he thinks everyone should be matched up, married and having kids."

"Unfortunately, not everyone has a happy ending. C'mon, let's check this place out," she said brightly, clearly wanting to drop the subject.

The cabin was quaint, and it had been aired and cleaned recently. They carried the groceries into the kitchen, which was small with outdated appliances.

"I think you'll be comfortable enough here for a few days."

"You aren't going to stay with me." It was a state-ment, not a question.

"I have work to do."

"Couldn't Siberia do it?"

"This is my case. I owe it to Stungun to see it through. It's my fault the man is dead."

"Don't say that. Of course it's not your fault. You're doing the best you can. We all are." She slid her arms around him and pressed her face into his neck. "For that matter, it's my fault, too. I obviously did something that gave me away to Mr. Vargov."

"No. He was already suspicious of you. You'd come to him with the problem first, remember."

"Well, there's no sense in rehashing. Let's move forward."

"To move forward, I have to catch the person responsible."

She sighed. "I know. I just wish we could have more time…" She sounded as if she wanted to say more, but she censored herself.

"More time for what?"

"For this." She kissed his neck, then opened two buttons on his shirt and kissed his chest.

"Ah, Lucy. What you do to me." He needed to leave. The sooner he took care of business, the sooner he could get back to her—and maybe figure out a way to be with her. But he couldn't bear just dumping her here and taking off.

He wanted—no, he *needed*—to be with her one last time, like he needed air to breathe.

Lucy thrilled at the way he responded to her touch. She'd never known she could have such a profound effect on a man, but his smooth skin quivered as she raked her palm down the muscles of his back, and his breathing came in ragged gasps as she touched her tongue to first one of his nipples, then the other.

There was no playful banter, no teasing. Bryan took her hand and led her up a flight of stairs, where she presumed bedrooms could be found. They entered one randomly. It was tucked up under the eaves with a window facing a breathtaking sunset. The old-fashioned iron bed had an antique quilt and half a dozen pillows covered in crisp, white cases.

Bryan undressed her slowly, paying special attention to each part of her he bared. Nothing escaped his attention—not her collarbone or the inside of her elbow or her ankle. Every place he touched her or kissed became an erogenous zone. Her senses were magnified so that she discerned the texture of his lips, the warmth of his breath against her skin, the sound of her own blood pounding in her ears.

She couldn't remember undressing him—maybe she was too engrossed in her own sensations to do it. But he ended up naked somehow, and he gently urged her onto the soft, much-washed cotton sheets, which smelled fresh, as if they'd just been pulled from the line, dried by wind and sunshine and put on the bed awaiting their arrival.

It was like making love on a cloud. The pillows were feather, and as they maneuvered on the bed, rolling this way and that, first Bryan on top, then Lucy, the pillows ended up surrounding them.

When he finally parted her legs and entered her, Lucy wanted to weep, she was so overwhelmed with the joyous sense of completion, the sense of rightness that this was where she belonged, with Bryan, in some dimension apart from embezzlers, terrorists and murderers. She wanted that more than she wanted her next breath. And as Bryan's strokes grew faster and harder, and warm rivers of sensation coursed through her limbs, coalescing into a cyclone deep in her center, she did cry.

Because this was goodbye.

He hadn't said it, but he didn't need to. He was leaving. And whatever happened, they wouldn't be together again. If he caught the traitors, they would no longer be a threat to her. She would return to her normal identity, get another job. She would cease to be Lindsay Morgan, Bryan's hot new girlfriend. And if the unthinkable happened, if he wasn't successful with his mission...

That alternative was too horrible to think about.

"Are you crying?" he asked a few minutes later, when their breathing had returned to something close to normal.

"No." But the tears were evident in her voice.

"Lucy, what's wrong?"

"Nothing. Oh, I'm just being silly. I know you're leaving. I know you have to. And I'm just scared of the future, that's all."

"Don't be scared. Siberia said he had a lead. We'll catch these guys, and I'll be fine, and I'll come back to get you and you'll be safe."

"Of course everything will work out," she said, feeling braver now that she heard the confidence in his voice. "I told you it was silly."

"I do have to go, though." His voice was tinged with regret.

"I know. But could you...could you just hold me until I fall asleep? And then slip away? I don't want to watch you leave."

"You are in a state, aren't you?" He laughed, but it was a soft, gentle laugh, filled with fondness. He slipped his arms around her and pulled her tight against him, drawing the sheet up over their naked bodies.

Lucy willed herself to relax, knowing if she didn't, Bryan would be waiting all night for her to fall asleep. As her muscles softened, one by one, tension turned to fatigue and she managed to drop off.

When next she woke, it was dark outside, the room slightly chilly. And she was alone, the space beside her cold. She turned on a lamp and checked her watch. It was after midnight. She saw then that Bryan had taken her little superspy phone from her purse and left it on a pillow with a note. The note instructed her to keep the phone with her, and what number to call if she had an emergency.

She shivered at the thought of that. Surely no one could find her all the way up here. All that was left for her to do was wait.

She thought she remembered Bryan leaving, putting on his clothes, lightly kissing her cheek. But maybe she'd only dreamed it. Because she also remembered him saying in a hoarse whisper, "I love you, Lucy."

Eleven

It was one of the few face-to-face meetings Bryan had had with Siberia. They met at a sidewalk café in D.C. the morning after he'd left Lucy. Each time his mind tried to wander to thoughts of her, to the way she looked when she slept, like a sexy fallen angel, he had to herd his attention back to the current time and place. If he and Siberia could solve this case, then he could think about Lucy all he wanted. Be with her, hold her, make love to her.

That was all the motivation he needed to stay focused.

"Vargov left a paper trail," Siberia said. He was an overweight man in his fifties who hadn't worked in the field in years due to an accident that had left him blind in one eye. His function was solely to coordinate intelligence. He wore a full, bushy beard, aviator sunglasses and a French beret, looking today more like an eccentric movie producer than a spy.

"He's in France," Siberia continued. "Tarantula is there now, coordinating with French intelligence agents. There's a very good chance Vargov will be apprehended. If you want to go there as insurance, it might be a good idea."

Bryan hesitated. He wanted to be where the action was. But the idea of going so far from Lucy made him uneasy. "I feel it's more important to protect our witness," he said.

"I could send a man—"

"No," Bryan said immediately. "I don't want another soul to know the location of that house. These guys— these terrorists, whoever they are—they're connected. The fact that they found Lucy the first time is nothing short of amazing. I still don't know where the picture was published."

"It was on a Britney fan site," Siberia said with a grimace. "I found it. Good disguise, by the way, but Ms. Miller's face was clear."

"So what's left?"

"Orchid."

Bryan was sick, thinking about his fellow agent-gone-bad. "I still can't believe it."

"I pray we're wrong. We won't know until we find her. I'm coordinating with the homicide investigators here. They think I'm CIA. I'll know more about the time and cause of Stungun's death soon."

"Who was he?" Bryan asked suddenly. "Surely it doesn't matter now." He couldn't stand the anonymity. He needed to put a real name to the man he'd known, a hometown, a family.

"I honestly don't know," Siberia said. "He was using one of the identities provided by the agency. I'm working through the chain of command to get more information. I'd like to be able to tell his family that he died defending his country—provided that's true. We still don't know. If he was dealing with terrorists, they've been known to turn on their own kind."

The thought sickened Bryan. Was this what he had to look forward to the rest of his life? Dealing every day with the scum of the earth, perhaps the worst of the scum his own supposed allies? Unable to trust anyone, not even his fellow agents?

Bryan knew then that he wanted out of this game. What had seemed exciting years ago was less than appealing now—the lying, the danger, the betrayals, the paranoia.

This was all Lucy's fault, he thought with a faint smile. She'd made him realize what was missing from his life—and what he very much wanted.

Lucy hadn't yet been at the cabin twenty-four hours and she was going stir-crazy. She'd explored every nook and cranny of the old house. There was a porch out back with a hammock, and she'd already had one nap. There was no TV, no radio, no way to keep in touch with the outside world. The highlights of her day so far had been a bowl of cereal for breakfast and a ham sandwich for lunch.

The scenery was breathtaking, and at any other time she'd have delighted in the views and the cool mountain breezes, a welcome respite from the heat of the city in the dead of summer. But she couldn't enjoy anything until she saw Bryan again, safe and sound. What had seemed an exciting lark when it started was now wearing on her nerves; she wanted it to be over. Now.

Mostly she wanted everyone out of danger. What if Vargov went after her family? But she also needed to know if what she and Bryan had shared was real, or merely a product of enforced proximity and too much adrenaline running through their veins.

Her feelings for Bryan felt very real to her, and he seemed to care for her beyond his responsibility of keeping her safe. But what did she know? She'd gotten it wrong before.

Whatever the results, she didn't want to live any longer in the fictional world of Lindsay Morgan. She needed to know if little Lucy Miller from Kansas had a chance with a superspy.

The idea seemed ridiculous, but she still hoped.

There was nothing to read in the house, not even a deck of cards to play with. How was she supposed to occupy herself? She finally decided to go for a run. Bryan had told her to stay put, but she would be no safer inside the house than out. The people who were after her weren't amateurs. Locked doors and windows would be no impediment if they really wanted her. At least if she was away from the house, she couldn't be cornered.

Besides, she'd gotten used to having a daily run with Bryan.

She donned her stylish shorts and matching tank top, thinking what a waste it was to sweat in such chic clothes when there was not a soul out here to see her. Thinking of Scarlet and her ban on T-shirts made her smile. Scarlet had been so good to her, and Lucy had started to think of her as a friend. Too bad she couldn't continue that friendship after Lucy and Bryan parted ways.

Taking the phone with her, Lucy stepped outside, locked the door, pocketed the key and set out at a brisk walk, continuing up the mountain road. She wondered how close to the top her cabin was, and if there was anyone else living up this way. She sure didn't see any signs of habitation, nor had she seen or heard a single car since she'd arrived. She'd thought the Catskills were more populated.

The uphill grade and uneven road surface made Lucy's run a challenge, but she pushed herself, figuring if she wore herself out, a shower and a nap might eat up the rest of the afternoon and it would be dinnertime. Finally, after about thirty minutes, she turned and headed back. The downhill trip was faster, and soon her cabin came into view.

She heard a car engine, and her heart beat faster. Bryan! Was it possible he'd resolved things so quickly? But she realized the car engine didn't sound like Stash's Peugeot, nor like Bryan's Jaguar. In fact, it sounded like a diesel car.

Reacting on pure instinct, she plunged into the heavy woods that surrounded the cabin, finding a vantage point where she could watch the road from behind a huge fallen tree.

She was probably being silly. It was no doubt some family on vacation, out for a drive. But soon the dark-blue Mercedes came into view, and she recognized it instantly.

Her heart beat double time and her skin, already flushed from her run, broke out in sweat. What was *he* doing here? How had he found her?

She pulled the phone from her pocket and carefully pushed the series of buttons that would put her in contact with Bryan. If Bryan was able to answer. Her imagination went into overdrive. What if Vargov had captured Bryan and tortured him into revealing Lucy's whereabouts?

The phone gave a series of beeps but nothing else. No ringing. No dial tone. No nothing. She tried again. Same beeps. Same nothing.

She whispered a curse. What was wrong with the phone? She was sure she was using it correctly. The battery was fine. But no calls would go through. Not even a call to 911.

What if Bryan was on his way back to the cabin this very minute? He would pull into the driveway, blissfully unaware that anything was wrong, and Vargov would kill him! She had to get down the mountain to the last little town they'd passed through—was it called Icy Creek?—where she could notify someone. And she had to make sure she met Bryan if he was headed this way. But to get past the cabin, she would have to go out in the open—or circle through the dense woods, way around.

As she dithered about what to do, the cabin's front door opened, and Vargov came out. He looked left, then right, scanning the woods. Her heart pounded. He was looking for her. He climbed into his car, and Lucy crossed her fingers. If he drove up the road looking for her, it would be her chance to get past the house. Sure enough, he headed up the mountain.

Just as she was about to make her move, she heard something, a loud something coming toward her, breaking branches and crunching leaves. Was it Vargov? Panic zinged through her. How had he found her so quickly? Did he have heat-seeking scanners? A tracking dog?

Then she realized it was not Vargov, and she didn't know whether to be relieved or not.

Because it was a black bear.

Okay, it would probably run if it saw her. Still, she

zipped up the nearest tree like a monkey, grateful for her rural upbringing. Her family had owned a small peach orchard, so she'd climbed her share of trees.

Wait a minute. Didn't bears climb trees?

It came closer. She was twenty feet up, well out of its reach, but it seemed to be very interested in her. It reared up on its hind legs and leaned up against the tree trunk, sniffing madly.

Oh, God, what if it started climbing? She considered screaming, but that would bring Vargov straight to her. Did she prefer to be shot, or eaten?

Just then there was another noise. The bear turned, wary of a threat. This time it was Vargov. He was quieter than a big man should be, hardly even crunching leaves, but she could hear his breathing. He'd probably parked the car up the road some place where it wouldn't be spotted so when she returned, she would assume all was well. Then, returning to the cabin on foot, Vargov had heard the bear and thought it was her.

Vargov and the bear saw each other at about the same time. The big man cursed and raised his gun, shooting at the hapless bear. He missed. The startled bear lumbered off at a gallop.

"Christ," Vargov muttered, still breathing hard and rubbing his neck. He was sweaty and pasty. "I'm too old for this."

He looked around, but he didn't look up. Lucy clung to her tree branch, the rough bark scraping her skin, the mosquitoes chomping on her, and prayed.

He holstered his gun and headed back toward the cabin.

Lucy waited until he'd gone inside, then clambered down. The business with the bear had wasted precious time. She'd lost her chance to get past the cabin. She would have to circle far around through the woods. But there was no other choice. She plunged into the thick undergrowth, getting slapped by twigs and branches, trying to be quiet in case Vargov had some listening device.

When she judged she was a good distance from the cabin, she headed downhill roughly parallel to the road, wondering how far she would have to hike before she reached Icy Creek.

Then she heard another car engine.

This time, to her horror, she recognized the distinctive rumble of Stash's Peugeot. She was still too far from the road to get there in time to head Bryan off. She broke into a run, heedless of the branches whipping at her face, hair and clothes. For a moment she thought she might beat him…but she was too slow. She broke cover just as the Peugeot turned into the cabin's driveway. The engine switched off and the driver's door opened.

"Bryan!" she called out. He froze, turned. "It's a trap!" She motioned frantically for him to get back in the car.

Her warning came too late. Shots rang out from the house. Bryan dived behind the car.

Lucy knew she should make for the safety of the woods. But all she could think about was being with Bryan again, facing the danger together. She made a headlong dash across the road toward the cabin. More shots came from the house, churning up the asphalt road inches from her feet. She expected one to rip through her flesh any moment. But by some miracle she made it to the car in one piece.

Bryan dragged her down beside him, then behind

him, placing his body between her and the shooter. "Lucy, are you crazy? You almost got killed."

"Yell…at me…later." She sucked in great gulps of air, feeling like she might pass out. "What do we do now?"

"Who's in the house?"

"Mr. Vargov."

"That's impossible. Vargov is in France."

"Don't you think I know my own boss?" she said impatiently. "It's definitely him. I took off into the woods, and a bear chased me, and then Vargov showed up and he shot at the bear—"

"Lucy, slow down. You're not making a lot of sense."

"Maybe we can outrun him," she said suddenly. "He's thirty pounds overweight and blind in one eye, so he has lousy depth perception."

"Maybe so, but he almost got— Did you say Vargov is blind in one eye? And overweight?"

"Yes. Didn't you know that?" She'd assumed he knew everything.

"Siberia is blind in one eye. And overweight. It's why he's not in the field anymore. Christ, Lucy, they're the same person."

Lucy let the implications sink in. No wonder Bryan had been having such a hard time with this case. His boss had been providing him with misinformation.

Bryan swore again and pulled his cell phone from his pants pocket. Almost instantly he realized it wouldn't work.

"Mine doesn't work, either," Lucy said. "I wanted to call you and warn you, but I couldn't."

"Vargov must have put a scrambler device in the cabin. It's why he lured us here—so we couldn't call for help."

"Then what do we do?"

Bryan silently reviewed their options. "We hold out until dark. We might stand a chance of making a break for it if Vargov can't see us."

But Vargov had no intention of allowing them to wait him out. Another flurry of shots rang out from the house. Bryan returned fire, breaking all of the upstairs windows. He practically sat on Lucy to keep her down and out of the line of fire.

When the shooting stopped, it was eerily quiet. Even the birds had stopped chirping, and the breeze had died to nothing.

"Maybe you got him," Lucy whispered.

"Doubtful." Bryan's voice had a strange, strangled sound to it. The hand he'd placed on her shoulder to keep her low to the ground lost its grip, and his gun rattled to the pavement.

"Bryan?"

He slumped against her, bleeding from a wound to the shoulder, dangerously close to his chest.

"Bryan!" In her panic, she forgot about the man shooting at them. Her only thought was that she would have to get Bryan some medical attention or he would die—and that meant getting him into the car and driving down the mountain.

He was conscious, though barely. "What—what are you doing?" he asked when she tried to hook her hands under his arms and lift him.

"You have to get into the car."

"Lucy, get down!" That was when she realized she'd been standing almost upright, and no one had shot at her.

Maybe Bryan had hit Vargov after all. Maybe he was reloading, or out of bullets altogether. She didn't have time to speculate. Bryan was bleeding at an alarming rate. The front of his shirt was soaked in red.

"You have to help me, Bry," she said. "You're too heavy. I can't lift you into the car myself."

Somehow, he managed to summon the strength to rise, casting a wary glance toward the house. But there was no more shooting. Lucy retrieved his gun, just in case, and together they hobbled to the Peugeot's passenger door. Lucy opened it, and Bryan fell inside.

The keys were in the ignition, thank God. She ran around, jumped behind the wheel, cranked up the car, backed out of the drive and screeched off. It was only when the cabin was half a mile behind them that Lucy dared to breathe a sign of relief. "We did it," she said, feeling only a mild sense of elation. One hurdle crossed, lots more to go. "Bryan?"

He was slumped in his seat, unconscious.

Twelve

The moment Lucy had reached Icy Creek, she tried her phone again, and it worked perfectly. She dialed 911, and in an astonishingly short time, tons of people came to her rescue. Two off-duty paramedics were summoned to administer emergency care to Bryan while arrangements were made to airlift him to the closest trauma center, Saint Francis Hospital in Poughkeepsie.

Someone had given her a map to Poughkeepsie, and Lucy had made it there in one piece only by the grace of God, because her mind wasn't on her driving. When she arrived, she could learn nothing about Bryan's condition other than that he'd still been alive when he'd arrived, and he'd gone almost immediately into surgery.

During the drive, which had seemed to take hours, Lucy had made a decision. Bryan was close to death, and she did not want him to die alone, with his family blissfully unaware of his condition. So she'd called first Daniel Elliott, then Amanda, then Scarlet. Bryan might not approve; explanations would have to be made, explanations Bryan would have just as soon skipped. But he would just have to be mad at her.

When his mother and father arrived, at virtually the same time, he was still in surgery.

"We couldn't wait," the young E.R. intern told them as they stood together, gripping each other's hands. It was the first time Lucy had seen Bryan's parents touch, or even acknowledge each other. "We'll let you know as soon as he comes out of surgery."

After the doctor walked away, Amanda's face crumpled. "I never thought we'd be facing this again," she said to Daniel.

Again? Lucy thought. Then she remembered about Bryan's childhood illness. He'd had high-risk surgery to correct his heart defect. His parents had probably spent more time than anyone should in hospital waiting rooms.

They both turned to her. "Lindsay, can you tell us more about what happened?"

"We were in a cabin in the Catskills," she said, choosing her words carefully. She didn't want to lie, not anymore. But she revealed only as much as she had to. "There was an intruder. He shot Bryan."

"How did you escape?" Amanda asked. "Did the intruder get away? Did you call the police?"

"I honestly don't know how or why I was spared," Lucy said, tears pressing hot and insistent behind her eyes. "All I remember is that I got Bryan into the car and got out of there. I contacted the authorities, but I don't know what happened to the man with the gun."

She hoped Vargov was alive. She wanted to testify and put him in jail for the rest of his life.

"I don't understand," Daniel said, giving Lucy a hard look. "First someone tried to kidnap you, then you had some kind of home invasion. Are you involved with criminals?"

"Not intentionally. I'm a material witness in a criminal case."

"But how does that involve Bryan?" Daniel wanted to know.

Amanda laid a quieting hand on her ex-husband's arm. "I should think that would be obvious, Daniel. Our Bryan is a spy."

Lucy gave a little gasp of surprise, but other than that she didn't confirm or deny.

"A what?"

"I should have put it together earlier," Amanda said. "The frequent absences, the injuries, the security measures at his apartment. And that phone of his—that's not an ordinary cell phone."

Daniel stared at Amanda in amazement. "You're telling me our son is a spy? How could you know that?"

"A mother knows these things," she said mysteriously.

Scarlet arrived with John, and then other Elliotts began trickling in. Some of them Lucy had met, some she hadn't. But apparently, when one of their own was threatened, they banded together, because she heard none of the bickering that had characterized previous family gatherings. There were lots of hugs and tears. Even the mysterious "Aunty Fin" showed up.

Lucy sat in a corner, feeling like the outsider she was, as Daniel and Amanda filled in family members as they arrived.

When two men in suits showed up, the mere sight of them filled Lucy with dread. They came straight for her, as she'd known they would.

"Ms. Miller?" one of them said.

Lucy rose and walked with them into a hallway, where the Elliotts couldn't hear the conversation.

They gave their names, claiming they were with the CIA.

"Listen, whoever you are, I don't care if you were sent by the president himself. I know you want me to go with you. I know you want me to tell you what happened. But frankly, I don't trust anyone right now. In the last forty-eight hours I've been almost kidnapped, shot at, and very nearly eaten by a bear. A United States agent tried to kill me—and he shot the man I love, who is in surgery right now fighting for his life. I'm not leaving here unless you remove me bodily from this hospital. I will report to the closest FBI field office tomorrow morning and give you and anyone who'll listen a full report. But not tonight. Is that clear?"

The two men looked at each other as they inched away from her. "Yes, ma'am." And, amazingly, they left. She wouldn't have believed that little Lucy Miller from Kansas, dressed in shorts and a tank top, could intimidate two federal agents, but apparently she had.

She returned to the waiting room to resume her vigil. Scarlet sidled up to her, giving her torn, filthy outfit, her messy hair and her scratched and scraped skin a disapproving look. "If fashion is a religion," she said solemnly, "you've broken virtually every commandment."

Bryan's first conscious feeling was one of panic. Shots fired. Pinned down. Pain, blood—then nothing.

Lucy! Oh, God, what had happened to Lucy? Was she dead or alive?

"Lucy," he mumbled.

Gradually sensation returned. Someone was holding his hand, but he couldn't quite summon the strength to open his eyes.

Next he became aware of sounds and smells. Alcohol. Betadine. Sterile sheets and beeping machines.

Suddenly he was ten years old again, coming out of surgery to repair his heart.

"Bryan? Are you awake?"

It was his mother squeezing his hand. Except he wasn't ten years old anymore. "Lucy," he said again. "Is Lucy okay?" He pried his eyes open to see both of his parents. "What are you doing here?" he asked, his voice sounding wispy and weak.

"Lindsay called us. How do you feel?"

Like his head was full of cotton and his chest full of knives. But he remembered how his mother felt every little pain right along with him, so he didn't tell her the truth. "I'm good," he said. And he was alive, at least, which was something. Then it sank in, what his mother had just said. "Lindsay" had called them. Lucy had at least made it off the mountain. "Is Lindsay okay?"

"She's got a few scrapes and bruises, but she's fine," Amanda assured him.

"What about me?" His body didn't feel normal, but he knew the surgical anesthesia always made him feel not quite connected to his body.

"You lost a lot of blood," Daniel answered. "The bullet nicked an artery, but it didn't hit any major organs. You'll be fine."

"And when you're fully recovered," his mother said

sweetly, "I'm going to kill you. Why didn't you tell us you were a secret agent?"

Uh-oh. His secret was out. Bryan supposed he should be surprised his perceptive mother hadn't put it together earlier. "'Cause you'd have grounded me."

Amanda's eyes filled with tears. "Oh, Bryan. We didn't go to all the trouble to get you heart surgery and save your life so you could throw it away chasing down terrorists and whatnot."

"Lucy—I mean Lindsay—told you everything?"

"She hardly told us anything," Amanda replied. "She said something about an intruder, that's all. But I put it all together. Bryan, I'm so angry with you." She sniffed back tears, and Daniel put his arm around her. "But I'm so proud, too."

It occurred to Bryan that this was the first time he'd seen his parents together like this since their divorce more than a dozen years ago.

"Where's Lucy?" he asked. "Hell. Lindsay—"

"We get the picture," Daniel said. "Lindsay is Lucy. She's in the waiting room. Two goons who looked like they could have been from the cast of *Men in Black* showed up wanting to take her away, but she got rid of them."

Bryan summoned a smile. That sounded like his Lucy. "Could you bring her here? I need to see her. I have to tell her—" Hell. He didn't know what he wanted to tell her. But if he could just see that she was okay, then he could handle the aftermath of this fiasco. And there was going to be a hell of an aftermath.

"I'll go get her," Amanda said. She patted Bryan's leg, then slipped out the door, leaving the two men alone.

"She's really special, this Lucy?" Daniel asked.

"More than you can know." Bryan shifted, trying to find a more comfortable position. The painkiller was wearing off, and the ache in his shoulder and chest were getting worse. "I don't know that we can— I mean, the only reason we were together—"

"If she's special, don't let her go," Daniel said solemnly. "No matter what anyone says. I'll let you rest now."

Bryan wanted to protest that he didn't need rest. He wanted to see Lucy. But he did nod off.

The next time he opened his eyes, she was there, sitting in a chair next to his bed. Someone had given her an old college sweatshirt to put on over her tank top. She was scraped and bruised, no makeup, her hair looking as if it hadn't seen a comb in some time. And she was the most beautiful woman he'd ever seen.

"Lucy?"

"I'm here."

"Sorry I'm not at my best."

"You're alive, which makes you exactly perfect in my book. And now you'll have a new scar to go with the others." She blinked back tears, proving she wasn't as cavalier as she was trying to be.

"You saved my life," he said. "There's no way to thank you."

She shrugged. "What else was I supposed to do? Anyway, there wasn't that much risk. Mr. Vargov is dead—that's why he stopped shooting at us. He apparently had a massive heart attack in the middle of trying to kill us."

"That was decent of him." At her stricken look, he immediately said, "Sorry. In my business, sometimes black humor gets us through tough times."

"I know he was a criminal and a traitor and a terrorist sympathizer, but I have a hard time equating that with the man I knew who was so kind to me. I shouldn't be sorry he's dead."

"You're allowed. Not everything is black-and-white, good and bad. Most criminals have some good in them. Who told you he was dead?"

"Orchid got in touch with me—she seems to be running things for the moment—but she didn't tell me much else. She said I should go home. Since Vargov's dead, she says I'm out of danger."

That was something Bryan would want to verify himself. "So you want to go home, then?"

She shrugged again. "Maybe I'll still have a job. The bank will need someone to help them restore those pension funds. I could get my umbrella back. I liked that umbrella."

Bryan thought for a long time before he responded to that. He thought about his longstanding rule to avoid commitments. He thought about how close he'd come to dying and how much he wanted to live to a ripe old age.

And he remembered what his father had said to him so recently, about not letting Lucy slip away. That was just what was going to happen if he didn't take a stand.

"What if I offered you another type of job?"

"What?"

"You have an uncanny talent for solving puzzles and finding patterns. Such skills are invaluable in intelligence work."

She looked at him like he was crazy. "You think I should become a spy?" she whispered.

"I was thinking more of a freelance consultant.

Working behind the scenes. I'll bet our government would even send you to code-breaking school."

Her eyes widened. "Really? I'd love that."

"And when you aren't working a case, you could help me with the restaurant. The place needs a female presence. People respond to you—you're a terrific hostess, you have good instincts when it comes to food…" He trailed off when he saw that he was not getting the response he'd hoped for. He'd been so sure she would love the idea. "You don't seem too enthusiastic."

"Oh, I would love the work, I'm sure. It's just—"

"You don't love me."

"Of course I love you. Oh, shoot, I wasn't going to say that. How pathetic is it, an accountant from Kansas falling for a millionaire superspy?"

Bryan couldn't breathe for a moment. This was better than he'd dared hope for. He thought maybe, if given more time, Lucy might be persuaded to fall in love with him. He'd never dreamed…

"If you're in love, why do you look so miserable? Haven't you figured it out yet? I want you to stay in New York because I'm head-over-heels crazy for you."

She brightened, but only for a moment. Then her eyes filled with tears. "I couldn't stand it, Bryan. I couldn't stand having you disappear with no explanation, not having any idea when you'd be back—or even *if* you'd be back. When I realized you'd been shot, I thought I was going to die myself. I'm not cut out to be a spy's girlfriend."

Bryan's heart swelled. He held out his hand. "Lucy, come here, please."

She did, though reluctantly, and he took her hand and squeezed it.

"If I was a little bit stronger, I'd pull you right into this bed with me, put my arms around you and never let you go."

"But—"

"No, no, hear me out. As of right now, I'm retiring. No more fieldwork. No more danger, no more unexplained trips abroad. No more lying to my family."

"But you…you love your work. You told me that yourself."

"It's exciting, yes. But staying alive is even more exciting. Particularly now that I have you to stay alive for. There are lots of other jobs I can do for the agency, or some other branch of the government. Intelligence gathering, sifting through data, coordinating efforts, debriefing agents, interviewing suspects—I'm trained to do all of that stuff. But I also want to spend more time at the restaurant. So we have lots of choices. If you stay in New York."

"Can I keep the clothes?" she asked, and he suspected she was trying to distract herself from actually having to answer him.

"I'll buy you all the clothes you want. Whoever that designer is who makes all those slinky dresses and whatnot, we'll go talk to him. Maybe he makes wedding dresses." He held tightly to her hand so she couldn't escape.

She used her other hand to muffle a shriek. "Bryan. Don't say things like that unless you mean it, it's cruel."

"You think I don't mean it? I want you to be my wife, Lucy. And frankly, if I don't marry you, my family is going to disown me. So, what do you say?"

"I think you're crazy." She tugged at her hand, but he refused to let her go. "This isn't how it's supposed to be!"

"I'll do the candlelight and violins as soon as they let me out of here. Put me out of my misery, Lucy."

In answer she leaned over the bed and kissed him, until one of the machines monitoring his vital signs started beeping out an alarm.

A nurse rushed into the cubicle. "What are you doing?" She angled a severe look at Lucy. "You, out."

Bryan kept hold of her hand. "Was that a yes?"

She nodded, her eyes filled with tears.

Two weeks later, on a hot day near the end of July, Lucy and Bryan were married at The Tides. Scarlet found her the perfect wedding dress, left over from a recent bridal spread *Charisma* had done. It was simple, with clean lines and unadorned silk. She paired it with an elegant pearl tiara.

Bryan sent Lucy's parents two round-trip, first-class tickets to New York, and though they'd never been out of Kansas in their lives, they came. They'd never even realized their daughter had gone missing. They'd called once, got her answering machine, figured she was traveling on some lark and put it out of their minds. Since they didn't know of her escapade, she didn't fill them in.

She didn't want them to spend the rest of their lives in church praying for her.

"You're not pregnant, are you?" her mother had whispered almost the moment she got off the plane.

Lucy laughed, amazed that she could. "No, Mom. I'm just in love."

"Well, I think you picked a good one this time. Have you ever traveled first class? Oh, my."

All of the Elliotts came for the wedding, even a few

more Lucy hadn't met. She still hadn't learned all their names.

Bryan closed down Une Nuit for the day and invited all the employees out to The Tides, except for the new busboys, who were now in jail.

Stash came, of course, driving his Peugeot, which now sported a few bullet holes. Bryan's employer had offered to repair the damage, but Stash enjoyed showing off the holes and bragging, to anyone who would listen, about his small part in the takedown of international terrorists. Lucy tried to steer her parents clear of him.

Bryan looked dashing as ever. The bandages on his shoulder hardly showed through his tuxedo, and he dispensed with his sling for the ceremony and the photos, but put it back on shortly after. He wasn't supposed to use his right arm while the tissues healed, but he claimed he wasn't in any pain.

The ceremony itself was short and sweet. Then there was the feasting, the way only restaurant people and Elliotts could feast. Chef Chin took over Maeve's kitchen like a general conquering a town. Maeve was more than happy to just get out of the way and enjoy the day.

The crowning glory of the reception feast was a four-layer cake, Bryan's little surprise for Lucy. She hadn't realized exactly what kind of cake it was until he fed her a piece of it for the photos.

Orange cake, garnished with chocolate and mint glaze. Not exactly traditional. But at the first taste, Lucy could feel her face heating—and other parts of her as well.

"Lucy, something wrong?" Bryan asked solicitously.

"I'm just having a Pavlovian response," she said, never imagining that orange cake could make her feel…amorous.

"I'm putting this cake on the menu, you know. Bryan and Lucy's Orange Wedding Cake."

She stood on her toes and whispered in his ear. "It would have been more appropriate as Bryan and Lucy's Honeymoon Cake."

"Don't worry, we'll take some with us."

Amanda, Bryan's mother, had arrived seconds before the ceremony, breathless and tense. Now he hugged her. "I was afraid you might not come, Mom."

"I wasn't about to miss my son's wedding—even if I do have to be under the same roof with *him*." She nodded toward Patrick, Bryan's grandfather.

This family had more drama and intrigue than a soap opera. But all families had their little issues, and Lucy vowed to accept them all as they came along. She reveled in the laughter, the smells and tastes of the day. She even enjoyed the family bickering, which they simply were not able to refrain from. She loved that she was now part of this crazy clan.

"You happy?" Bryan asked Lucy quietly as they posed for yet more pictures.

"Deliriously."

"You should be afraid. Very afraid."

"Because…?"

"You fit in perfectly. You've become an Elliott."

Lucy could think of nothing more wonderful.

* * * * *

THE ELLIOTTS *continues next month*
With *MARRIAGE TERMS by Barbara Dunlop.*
Don't miss the continuing family saga,
available in August from Silhouette Desire.

Silhouette® Desire

Stability is highly overrated....

Dana Logan's world had always revolved around her children. Now they're all grown up and don't seem to need anything she's able to give them. Struggling to find her new identity, Dana realizes that it's about time for her to get "off her rocker" and begin a new life!

Off Her Rocker

by Jennifer Archer

HARLEQUIN®
NeXt™

Silhouette Desire

COMING NEXT MONTH

#1741 MARRIAGE TERMS—Barbara Dunlop
The Elliotts
Seducing his ex-wife was the perfect way to settle the score, until the Elliott millionaire realized *he* was the one being seduced.

#1742 EXPECTING THUNDER'S BABY—
Sheri WhiteFeather
The Trueno Brides
A reckless affair leads to an unplanned pregnancy. But will they take another chance on love?

#1743 THE BOUGHT-AND-PAID-FOR WIFE—
Bronwyn Jameson
Secret Lives of Society Wives
She'd been his father's trophy wife and was now a widow. How could he dare make her his own?

#1744 BENDING TO THE BACHELOR'S WILL—
Emilie Rose
Trust Fund Affairs
She agreed to buy the wealthy tycoon at a charity bachelor auction as a favor, never expecting she'd gain so much in the bargain.

#1745 IAN'S ULTIMATE GAMBLE—Brenda Jackson
He'll stop at nothing to protect his casino, even partaking in a passionate escapade. But who will win this game of seduction?

#1746 BUNKING DOWN WITH THE BOSS—
Charlene Sands
A rich executive pretends to be a cowboy for the summer—and finds himself falling for his beautiful lady boss.